BITTER AUTUMN

Returning to New Zealand from Canada, Russ Gallagher becomes involved in a dangerous venture to recover a large quantity of illegally mined gold. Travelling to the Bay of Islands in pursuit of two American visitors who he believes have hidden the precious metal, he discovers he has been deliberately misled. Gallagher arranges to smuggle the gold to Los Angeles, but his plans to follow are complicated by unexpected events, forcing him into a desperate situation . . .

COLIN D. PEEL

BITTER AUTUMN

Complete and Unabridged

LINFORD
Leicester

First published in Great Britain in 1973 by
Robert Hale Limited
London

First Linford Edition
published 2003
by arrangement with
Robert Hale Limited
London

British Library CIP Data

Peel, Colin D. (Colin Dudley), *1936* –
Bitter autumn.—Large print ed.—
Linford mystery library
1. Detective and mystery stories
2. Large type books
I. Title
823.9'14 [F]

ISBN 0–7089–9954–9

Published by
F. A. Thorpe (Publishing)
Anstey, Leicestershire

Set by Words & Graphics Ltd.
Anstey, Leicestershire
Printed and bound in Great Britain by
T. J. International Ltd., Padstow, Cornwall

This book is printed on acid-free paper

For
Julienne

1

The bright sunshine didn't fool me for a minute. Even though it was warm, I knew from bitter experience that the weather could break at any time.

Last weekend was Labour Day, which was the time of year that the east coast Canadians take down the bug screens and fit their double windows. I've always thought it a sort of ritual, an unpleasant one to me. Once Labour Day is past I wait with dread for the first icy fingers of winter to creep across Montreal.

But this time I was going to beat the cold, not really through choice but through having a good enough excuse to leave my job, leave Montreal and leave Canada.

The taxi pulled up outside the International Passenger Air Terminal amidst a crowd of people staggering with their luggage leaving the early morning down town bus.

1

I grabbed my single suitcase from the seat beside me, put a five dollar bill into the hand of the driver and stepped onto the sidewalk.

A hundred memories — or at least three years' worth — came bubbling up from inside me. Montreal is a good place to live and Canada is an easy place to like or even fall in love with. Perhaps I was doing the wrong thing — but it was too late now.

I joined the queue at the Air Canada counter and went mechanically through the paperwork. Immigration and customs clearance for passengers to the United States are carried out before you leave Canada. I've always thought that it was a particularly good system. Getting everything over before you leave is very much better than the frustration that always results from hanging about for hours at your destination.

With my papers stamped, stapled and nicely arranged in the free Air Canada plastic wallet, I walked slowly to the 707 loading ramp. I could see people filtering into the front hatch of the fuselage.

Once seated inside I pulled out the telegram from my shirt pocket. The yellow paper had begun to tear at the folds it had been opened so often.

Automatically I read it again, knowing it was impossible to read anything new into the few simple words. Every time I did this I got the same feeling.

I closed my eyes and tried to remember Karen.

The big turbines began to whine. The seat belt notice must be on but I didn't care. Nobody shook me so I guess they figured that the take-off would be okay. That was something.

The thrust of acceleration forced me to open my eyes again — probably because I was frightened. I always become a bit jittery during take-off.

Through the window on the far side of the fuselage I could see Dorval rushing by. Three years of my life streamed past the plexiglass hole in horizontal stripes of different colour, changing finally to a pale blue as the jet left the ground and began to climb.

My hand that held the telegram was

sticky. I read it again.

'Russ stop Boyd missing 12 days Coromandel Can you come home at once please stop Please letter follows Karen.'

It was dated October 3rd, 1971. Today was the tenth, more than long enough for an airmail letter to have reached me if she had mailed it the same day that the cable had been sent.

I looked out of the window.

Far below, the vastness of Canada spread out a magnificent tapestry of lakes and green forests. Soon it would all be white and a lot less interesting.

'Coffee?' I smiled at the passing hostess.

She nodded without stopping.

I sat watching the ground creep by beneath with unseeing eyes.

Why after all this time had Karen cabled me? I hadn't heard a single word from her since I left Auckland in 1969. I hadn't expected to. When she married Boyd I didn't anticipate letters saying how happy they both were and how well things were going for them — assuming things had gone well. Anyway I didn't care — or thought I didn't.

Of course I had thought vaguely of going west for the winter, either to Seattle or San Francisco to miss the cold, but I certainly hadn't planned to go home. There was nothing there for me. Or there hadn't been until now.

The coffee arrived together with two small cookies on a plastic tray, interrupting my thoughts momentarily.

Karen wouldn't have cabled me unless something serious had happened I was sure. There were plenty of other people who she could turn to if there was trouble of some kind. Why me?

I was tired of trying to figure it out.

Leaving my job hadn't been hard. I'm an aeronautical engineer and aircraft contracts are at best precarious in Canada. Whilst you work you make money — big money — but when the contracts are over — out you go. The joint U.S./Canadian fighter bomber that I'd been working on for the last eighteen months was not economically feasible and both Governments knew it. A couple more months of study would have put the last nail in the coffin of the N.A. 52 project. There was nothing to follow it that I knew of either. It would have meant a move to Ottawa or perhaps even to the States or Europe. I had forestalled the obvious — that was all.

Leaving Montreal and my friends was not so easy, even though it was probably inevitable. You can quite enjoy a Canadian winter if you have the right company and I certainly had that.

My first winter had been pretty awful because I didn't really know enough people. Also I tend to be a bit shy. People do not readily like me at first — I think it takes a long time for them to see through what is an obviously unattractive surface. By summer though I was firmly accepted by a group of friends whose company I enjoyed, and I forgot Karen and forgot New Zealand.

Now the memories of my homeland started to come back again. Once in a while I used to think of the softness of that far away country — mostly when freezing cold in downtown Montreal. I realised I had begun to reminisce.

I'm not entirely sure if I'm a bastard or not. All I know is that I believe I was one of those unwanted babies that are born to unmarried mothers. That was thirty-one years ago now and doesn't have much to do with the story of Russ Gallagher. I don't even know where I got my name from. It's never worried me and I'm not one of those guys who are always wondering who their parents were.

When I was sixteen I was one of the lucky few who got a Cadetship with Air New Zealand to study aeronautical engineering at Auckland University. That's where I met Karen. Not that she was studying aeronautical engineering — I can't imagine her doing that.

Karen Wendle — as she was then — was taking history. I knocked her down gently with my car one afternoon as I was leaving. Karen must have been about nineteen I suppose and I was twenty-two, in my last year.

It turned out to be a very minor

accident but one of the luckiest I've ever had — at least I thought that once.

Right from the beginning Karen and I had something which many people go through life never having. It was the nearest thing to a permanent holiday that I can imagine, and it lasted for five whole long full years.

Then I went to Australia to make my fortune so that we could get married. Boyd, Boyd Hallett appeared on the Auckland scene whilst I was away, and in eleven months married the girl who had made my entire life into something meaningful.

Sure I was bitter. I hated Boyd and I hated Karen so much that I ached for her in self-pity. It was a hell of a time for me. So I went to Montreal.

I guess it all sounds pretty uninteresting. I don't talk about it much. It all happened a long time ago now and the hurt lasted less than a year but I would still cut off my arm for Karen Wendle, even though I'm not in love with her or her memory any more.

Aircraft are good places to think in — I

don't get bored like some people — I like having time to think. On this occasion it seemed like a good opportunity to think of Russ Gallagher and what he was going to do with his life from now on.

One thing was certain. I was going to have a darned good look at New Zealand and get a lot of hunting in whilst I was about it.

Reaching for my flight bag I extracted the new catalogues of hunting equipment that I'd picked up yesterday. I had been promising myself a brand new rifle for about a year, and I was looking forward to buying one in San Francisco during my stop over there.

The last thing I can remember is flicking through the pages.

* * *

Of course it was still early when we arrived in San Francisco and the sunshine didn't look any different through the window to the Montreal kind three thousand miles away.

An announcement came over the

speakers saying that the temperature was sixty-eight degrees — colder than it was in Montreal. So much for California.

We touched down seven minutes early.

Peter was waiting for me at the glass door inside the terminal. It was good to see him.

My cheap old suitcase was on the top of the pile that had already been taken off the merry-go-round baggage dispenser by the more energetic passengers.

I lifted it easily, marched to the exit and was pumping the big hand of my old friend Peter Crittall before I knew it.

'How are you — you old ratbag?' he grinned at me.

He looked a bit older, a little more grizzled around the mouth. I didn't say anything — I was too pleased.

He said, 'Come on, the car's outside.'

It was some car, a battered white Lotus Cortina which he drove with extreme enthusiasm. After a few minutes I fastened the seat belt.

'I didn't have to use one of these on the plane,' I complained.

'You getting old, Russ?'

'Old and careful.'

He gave me another huge grin as we screamed off the El Camino Real main highway turning up towards the hills on the way to Half Moon Bay.

Peter said, 'There's a letter for you from Karen.'

'In that case, Mr. Crittall will you please get this heap out of first gear and move — I need to read that letter very badly.'

I was excited — unreasonably so. Karen must have bargained on me leaving Montreal as soon as I could and had guessed that I'd call on Peter and Bev on the way over.

In less than twenty minutes we were turning into the long gravel driveway of the modest eighty thousand dollar Crittall property.

Bev came rushing out as the engine of the poor Lotus spluttered to a halt. I braced myself.

'Russ — Russ Gallagher you.'

The impact was as bad as I expected. I staggered under the embrace.

I said, 'Hi Beverly,' and tried to unwind myself.

She was out of breath with excitement.

'Gee it's great to see you, Russ.'

'It's only been three years, Bev.'

'Only! he says, Peter.'

We walked to the house with Beverly making welcome noises all the way.

I ate my way steadily without enjoyment through an enormous brunch — just to please her.

Peter and Bev had been close friends of Karen and I in the old days in Auckland. They had married in California and had been here ever since. Peter has a very successful electronics company in San Carlos. Both of them are as happy as the days are long and always have been. I envied them a lot.

I'd last seen them on the way over to Canada. I stayed for two weeks then. Of course they'd heard about Karen and Boyd and tried to be kind to me. I couldn't stand it. This time it really was nice to see them again.

Beverly gave me Karen's letter as soon as we finished eating.

Peter said, 'I thought you were in a hell of a hurry to read it.'

'I am, but I didn't want to be impolite.'

'Read it.'

It started off by saying that she was sorry that she hadn't managed to get a letter off to Montreal at once but she couldn't. But she didn't say why. It went on to explain that she had already asked Peter to forward this letter to Canada if I didn't turn up in San Francisco.

It was still rather disjointed but the essence of the story was clear and not a little disturbing.

Apparently, last May, Boyd had met some people in Auckland who had persuaded him to join a highly speculative and illegal mining venture on the Coromandel Peninsula. Boyd was a qualified geologist so I guess that's how he became involved in something like that. Even so, from what I knew of him he wasn't the kind of guy to take any stupid risks.

The detail was pretty thin and Karen's writing was certainly not the best.

As far as I could determine, the deal had progressed quite well to the point where the samples of rock that Boyd had brought back to Auckland for analysis looked exciting.

Then in late September, some six months after the whole thing had started, Boyd failed to return after an unscheduled trip into the mine.

Karen and her brother David had tried to make contact with Boyd's partners but couldn't trace either them or the mine. It seemed that Karen had a fair idea of where the mine was but, not surprisingly, they hadn't been able to obtain any indication of what had happened to her husband.

On September the twenty-eighth Boyd's dog was found wandering along a sheep trail in the high country with a bad bullet wound in its back.

David wouldn't let his sister contact the police — which was probably a smart decision where illegal mining was concerned.

I had decided by now that Boyd must have been after gold. What I couldn't figure out is how anybody with Boyd's experience could believe you could get any reasonable quantity of gold out of Coromandel.

All of the yellow metal that had ever been mined there had been in the form of ore that had to be crushed before the gold could be extracted from it. Even then it wasn't easy. At least as far as I knew that was the way it was done. Nobody could possibly set up the necessary equipment nowadays and hope to keep it secret for very long. The whole thing sounded faintly unbelievable.

Abruptly the letter finished by saying that Karen thought Boyd was in serious trouble and that David had recently gone into the bush alone to try to find him.

On October the third she had become so concerned having heard nothing from her brother that she had cabled me.

And that was that. The letter was signed 'Love Karen'.

Bev and Peter were staring at me across the table when I looked up.

Peter said, 'Well?'

'Trouble.'

'Karen and Boyd?'

'Boyd's missing in the bush on Coromandel.'

'That's no reason to cable you,' Beverly sounded indignant on my behalf.

'They're mixed up with an illegal mine.'

Peter said, 'Oh Christ!' and reached for the bottle of wine that we had opened to celebrate our reunion.

Beverly said, 'So Mrs. Hallett cables good old Russ Gallagher and he comes running.'

Peter said, 'It is a bit off don't you think?'

'Wouldn't you help her?' I asked them.

They both nodded at me slowly.

I grinned at my friends.

I said, 'Maybe the bastard's dead,' but added quickly. 'I'm only kidding. I'm not carrying a torch for Karen anymore — she's just one of the closest friends I'll ever have — like you two.'

Peter said, 'Do you want me to come?'

I knew he would and I knew he didn't have time to.

'Are you suggesting I am not capable of sorting out the mess, Mr. Crittall?'

He was looking worried — rather like a Saint Bernard dog.

I said, 'Come on, run me down town. I have some shopping to do, and you have to show me San Francisco again and tonight we are going to get high.' Which is exactly what we did.

2

I had decided to fly out on the four o'clock plane via L.A. and Hawaii. Although I wouldn't admit it, I was very anxious to get home, anxious to see Karen and in a curious way eager to help her find Boyd. Peter and Bev understood I know.

In the corner of the room the new hunting rifle I'd bought yesterday sat in its box still half-wrapped in its rust-proof paper. It was a model 62 lever action Marlin chambered for .256 Winchester magnum. In experienced hands this little rifle would be capable of killing the toughest wild animal anywhere in the world. In New Zealand I hoped to shoot wild pig. I'd hunted before in Northland back home, and a lot in Canada for bear and deer, but I had never been on a pig hunt. I hoped there would be plenty of opportunities when I got home — after I'd sorted out Karen's problems.

Shortly after lunch I said good-bye to Beverly at the house, waving to her as Peter drove me down the driveway.

We didn't speak much in the car.

At the airport he said, 'If there's real trouble — you call me.'

'It'll be okay.'

'If it is what will you do?'

I patted my rifle case. 'Go bush for the summer, lie on beaches and be a bum.'

He looked envious for a moment. I could even feel the tingle of enthusiasm in myself as I said it. We shook hands.

I said, 'I'll keep in touch, Peter,' and walked quickly into the building.

The fifteen hundred mile flight to Los Angeles was enjoyable, mainly because the dry hills of California are so wonderful from the air. The barrenness and obvious dryness of everything contrasts with the lake-covered terrain of eastern Canada and made the New Zealand of my memories as green as I imagined Ireland to be. The northern part of New Zealand can get very dried up at the end of summer, but nothing like southern and central California in October.

Smog lay over Los Angeles as mist lies over Auckland in early autumn, except that this was evil in colour. The word blanket describes it almost perfectly. It took over half an hour from the time the plane entered the edge of the cloud to the time that we landed. I'm glad I don't live there.

At L.A. the plane filled up with passengers, most of them returning to Hawaii by the look of them. The aircraft was a DC Super 8 with seven channels of music to choose from and with two movies, but time passed slowly despite the entertainment; I was beginning to become keyed up about Karen.

Half-way through the movie my concentration failed me so I turned my stereo earphones to the classical music tape, closed my eyes and tried to plan what I would do when I arrived in Auckland.

Karen had thoughtfully neglected to provide any instructions on how I was to contact her, when, and if I turned up in New Zealand. Almost certainly the post mark on the letter was my best bet. It had been sent from the little mining town of Coromandel itself, in the heart of the great peninsula. I'd been there several times. If I hired a car and drove from Auckland, I thought I should be able to find her fairly easily.

★ ★ ★

We landed in Auckland at exactly eight o'clock.

I walked out into a clean smelling Pacific morning, glad to have my journey over and very glad to be back.

Customs were interested in my rifle, but no more than interested. It had cost me one hundred and eighty American dollars so I had half-way anticipated trouble — but there was none.

A taxi took me into Papatoetoe where I rented a Volkswagen — the beetle kind. My suitcase and rifle would just fit across the small back seat.

To my left, the sun was beginning to climb into the clear North Island sky as I turned onto the southern motorway. I had just travelled eight thousand miles to rescue the husband of a girl I used to think was the whole world, and I was strangely elated — as if on the edge of something important. It was a pleasant feeling.

This was the first time I had ever completed a transcontinental flight without sensing either the immediate need to establish a base and pause for thought, or recover from the hours spent in an unnatural environment. There was no need for that this time. I wanted to see Karen, to show her that I'd come when she called — to show her that our five years together still meant something. There was no suggestion of the old attraction — just the need to assist a very close friend who had cried out in the night for me.

New Zealand was beautiful. More beautiful than I remembered — much more. Hungrily I gulped in the scenery as I sped along up over the Bombay Hills before turning off at Pokeno on the road to Thames.

The odd milk tanker and tractor appeared suddenly around corners to be left behind as quickly as I came upon them. Fern and cabbage trees dotted the slopes everywhere, vegetation that I'd forgotten. Huge clumps of flax and rolling sheep paddocks grazed to a green velvet carpet lined the side of the road.

The land sparkled with freshness and cleanness rather like Canada on a bright winter's morning without the snow and oh so much softer and much different really. I ached with pleasure to be home.

As I approached Thames the country became flatter, the road being almost completely straight, although the surface was absolutely awful.

In front of me the Coromandel range rose magnificently into the sky, looking a little foreboding and evil. It had no similarity with anything I'd seen either in Australia or Canada, although there are plenty of places in New Zealand that are pretty much the same. I could recall some but none as impressive.

Now my Volkswagen was buzzing along Highway 2 right at the bottom of the Hauraki Gulf — at the southern tip of the Firth of Thames. I crossed the Piako

River, then the larger Waihou before turning north on the coast road to Thames.

Suddenly I was on the outskirts of town, rattling over railway lines along a street lying parallel to what seemed to be the main centre. Turning up towards the busier street I noticed a small coffee bar on the corner. I pulled up, thankfully uncoiling myself from the cramped confines of the Volkswagen. My six foot frame has never fitted well into small European cars.

A couple of local inhabitants were arguing at one of the four tables. The New Zealand accent, drawl, or whatever you care to call it, sounded very pronounced to my acquired Canadian ears. It was difficult not to listen.

'Coffee with cream and a packet of cigarettes,' I said to the Maori girl who appeared from a door behind the counter.

After careful study during the latter part of my life I've found that long shots pay off a lot more often than you would expect.

I said, 'I'm looking for a Mrs. Hallett

24

— I don't suppose you have any idea where I might find her?'

The girl shook her head as she passed me the cigarettes.

She said, 'There's a hotel along the way.'

So much for long shots.

One of the natives walked towards me, following me to the table.

I nodded good morning to him.

'Gidday,' he said.

That sounded familiar. I said, 'Gooday.'

'Did you say Hallett?' he asked.

My pulse quickened slightly.

He was a typical Kiwi. The crinkles at the corners of his eyes, etched in white where the sun had been kept out, and the dirty denim shorts, branded him as surely as if he had worn the N.Z. emblem on the pocket of his open necked shirt.

I said, 'Mrs. Karen Hallett.'

He took the cigarette I offered him.

'There was something about a Hallett in the paper a couple of days ago,' he said slowly. 'Coromandel it was.'

'What was?'

'Hallett.'

I drank my coffee watching him over the cup.

The effort proved too much. He shook his head. 'Just remember the name that's all.'

'But it was in Coromandel.'

'Yis, oh yis.'

I said, 'Thank you, I'll drive up there then.'

'Just keep on up the coast.'

'Yeah, I know — thanks again.'

I left him sitting at the table trying to remember.

A lot could have happened since Karen had written the letter she'd sent to California. For the name Hallett to have appeared in the paper something serious must have happened. Unless of course Karen had simply notified the authorities that Boyd was missing. That seemed the most likely explanation.

Coromandel is about twenty-five miles north of Thames. Although I couldn't remember exactly what the road was like, I figured that it would take me less than an hour no matter how bad it was. In fact for New Zealand the road was pretty good as far as the surface was concerned.

I suppose it is a very scenic drive. Even though I was now trying to make time, I just couldn't help slowing now and again when the road swept down to almost sea level next to a particularly unspoilt beautiful rocky bay. The road followed the coast so exactly that the Firth of Thames was continually displayed to my left, allowing me to see clear across to the Hunua range south of Auckland city.

The sea was incredibly calm. Mostly the sun had only recently reached the little beaches which lay in the shadow of the hills, and the water was blue right out across the Gulf.

Consisting mostly of holiday cottages, I passed through the little coastal townships of Te Puru, Waiomu and Tapu. At Wilsons Bay the road curved inland, and began to climb, providing absolutely stupendous views into the sheltered bays some seven or eight hundred feet below. This part of the road I remembered quite well — I wasn't far from Coromandel now.

If Karen's name had reached the

newspapers it was going to be even easier to find her than I had hoped. Of course there was no guarantee that she would still be there — it all depended on the events of the past few days.

Only minutes away I began to get cold feet. Would she kiss me hello, or should we shake hands? Was I as close a friend to Karen as she was to me? I suppose she wouldn't have cabled me unless she still felt something. How would I feel when I saw her?

I tried not to think about our imminent meeting. I'd just let it take its own course and see how it went. Anyway I wasn't in love with her anymore. I realised that I'd become tired of telling myself that. Karen had been married for three years which would have changed her I knew — and what about the Canadian girls I'd lived with. Who was I kidding?

The yellow signpost said Coromandel one and a quarter miles. I stubbed out the cigarette, pushed the accelerator to the floor and shut off my mind completely.

Coromandel was quite busy. Cars and several Land-Rovers were puttering about the outskirts, and there were a few well used tractors about. I didn't know where to stop so I pulled up outside a large white weatherboard building, reminiscent of some of the older Canadian architecture I had seen in Quebec. It was a hardware store.

Behind me a very battered Land-Rover Safari clattered to a stop, parking too close to the rental Volkswagen.

The fresh faced young man that stepped out looked slightly embarrassed as I inspected the two inch gap between our bumpers with exaggerated interest.

I said, 'I've just driven down from Auckland — I'm looking for a Mrs. Hallett whom I believe is in Coromandel.'

The boy looked awkward. 'Are you a relation, mister?'

'No, a friend — do you know where I could find her?'

'It's the first left up there,' he pointed.

I wished I hadn't made a thing out of his parking. I'd meant it to be a joke.

Walking up the street my feet wouldn't keep at a steady pace. I turned the corner to find a small crowd of people gathered on the sidewalk.

A converted Chevrolet hearse was parked on the other side of the road. There was a flower-covered coffin in the back.

Karen stood with her back to me, her long dark hair tied behind her head with a ribbon. I could have told it was Karen from twice the distance.

When I was fifteen feet away I said, 'Karen.'

She spun round.

She said, 'Oh Russ,' and suddenly was in my arms sobbing.

I stood uncomprehending trying to catch hold of my emotions.

I was still struggling when someone tapped me on the shoulder and said, 'Hi Russell.'

I turned. It was Boyd.

3

I guess the surprise must have shown all over my face. There was no doubt that I was very confused indeed. From the time that I'd walked around the corner of the street, my mind had been in turmoil trying to understand what the hell was going on.

Not unreasonably I had concluded that Boyd Hallett must have been recovered dead after being missing in the bush. Karen's reaction — and her obvious grief confirmed these suspicions.

Then, after sorting all this out in perhaps less than fifteen seconds I had been confronted by Boyd, who was obviously very much alive.

He'd lost a lot of weight since I'd seen him last and he looked rather pale and tired.

I didn't know Boyd well. We'd met several times before I left for Montreal but I had no real impression of what sort of guy he was.

He shook my hand with what appeared to be genuine enthusiasm.

I said, 'To coin a phrase I thought this was your funeral Boyd.'

Karen said, 'Not Boyd's, Russ — David's.'

Now I understood. 'Your brother!'

'He was twenty-three years old,' she said bitterly.

'What happened?'

'Shot through the head.'

Boyd interrupted us. He said quickly, 'This isn't the place to talk about it Russell, we'll explain later after the funeral's over.'

Karen said, 'Boyd and I will go with David and meet you afterwards at the hotel, Russ.'

Boyd said, 'There's only one, two streets up from this.'

I nodded my agreement, I needed breathing space.

With real regret I said, 'Karen, I'm terribly sorry about your brother.'

She looked hard at me for a while.

She said, 'You have no idea what it means to me that you came all the way from Montreal because I asked you to.'

I'd been wondering if I was really wanted now that Boyd had returned safely. David's death must be concerned with the mining business and quite obviously the matter was far more serious than I had imagined; even so, Karen mightn't want me to interfere now.

I said, 'I'll be at the hotel — I'll see you there.'

The funeral seemed to be badly organised. Various people were still milling about in the road when I left.

I recalled the expression on the face of the young man in the Land-Rover as I walked back to the car. David's death must have been big news in Coromandel. His sister's name would have been seen in the paper by the man I had spoken to in Thames. I wondered what the police were doing about it.

The Land-Rover was gone. I drove the Volkswagen slowly to the hotel. Besides the Halletts, I was the only guest the receptionist told me. She also told me how lucky I was because they only had three rooms at the moment. Usually there were five, but two were being redecorated.

I made the right noises at the right time in between her chatter as she took me up the wooden stairs to my room.

'Dinner at seven,' she said finally.

'Thank you.'

She went — still talking but I wasn't listening any more, there was too much on my mind.

The window of my room afforded a splendid view of some steep hills on the west side of the peninsula. What the hell had been going on up there, I wondered.

In frustrating situations like this there is only one answer. I went downstairs and bought a whole carton of canned beer which I carried back to my room. A pleasant surprise was the opener fixed to the inside of the lid — that saved another trip.

I opened a can and stripped the cellophane from a new pack of cigarettes. Then, having prepared myself for some heavy thinking, I lay on the bed with both hands behind my head and closed my eyes.

About half an hour later, when I was ready for some more beer, there was a knock at the door.

Boyd followed Karen into the room. He was limping badly.

I opened three more beers giving one to each of my visitors.

They looked at me.

With care I said, 'I have travelled three quarters of the way round the world at great expense and with great discomfort to help a girl I once knew who was or is in trouble. I do not expect gratitude but I am not going to give you any more beer unless you talk to me.'

Before Boyd could say anything I held up my hand to stop him.

'I haven't finished my speech. I'm quite sure that you've decided that you are not going to tell me anything — even though you both feel awful about dragging me away from my skiing. Please allow me to make it absolutely clear that I intend becoming involved whether you want me to or not. Three years ago — or three years plus a bit — Karen and I were engaged to be married, until you, Boyd, came along and loused the whole thing up, at least for me you did. A lot has happened to me since then. I guess a lot has happened to you too, and poor David is dead. You have got Russ Gallagher here and you are damn well stuck with him.'

My speech might not have been particularly eloquent but I hoped that I might just have mixed enough humour with seriousness to do the job. The recent funeral made it difficult to be too funny.

Boyd said, 'I'm sorry about the air fare.'

I sat up on my bed. Predictably it squeaked loudly.

'And I don't want your rotten money!'

I looked at Karen. I said, 'For God's sake Karen I was a close friend of David's — don't those five years mean anything to you?' I was starting to get angry.

Boyd wouldn't meet my eyes and Karen began to cry softly. She looked very helpless.

In exasperation I fell back on the pillow with unnecessary violence. 'Talk,' I shouted.

Boyd said, 'Okay Russ — take it easy.'

He stood up taking a couple more cans of beer from the carton.

It was going to be all right. For a few minutes I'd been quite worried. Now I relaxed and waited.

He began. 'As you probably know, Russ, I'm a geologist. That means that either I can make a large quantity of money easily or starve. Good geologists are paid huge sums by big organisations — especially the oil companies, but there are plenty of us that scratch along doing the odd contract and probably never will make the big time.

'Karen and I had a decent living, I suppose, but I've always thought that I should be able to do better than that, and I'm the sort of joker that always keeps his ear to the ground, hoping for some good news.

'Anyway, last May, I was having a beer in a bar in Auckland one lunch time — I'd been in town to wind up a small contract I'd been doing in Whangarei. There were a couple of Americans there who started talking to me. They'd been in New Zealand for the game fishing up in the Bay of Islands over the summer, and had been down touring round the Gulf before going home to the States.

'We chatted about this and that, and somehow or other the fact that I was an out of work geologist came out. In fact I'd only been out of work for a couple of hours, but future prospects weren't good so I was unemployed really. The conversation turned to the old mining days up here in Coromandel and we all speculated, like everyone else does, about the chances of making a little on the side up in the hills.'

For the next hour or so Boyd talked steadily, recounting his increasing involvement with the two American visitors.

It transpired that they had attempted to reopen a derelict mine in the hills near the Waitaia peak, across on the east coast of the peninsula.

Both men came from Seattle in Washington and knew a little about mining — enough to make Coromandel very interesting to them. Originally they'd heard of the mine from a local they'd met on a weekend tramping trip. He was about seventy years old, and subsequently had been hired as a general odd job man and caretaker for the mine.

The first thing was to get some decent air into the hole and drain it properly. Working by themselves, polythene ducting had been progressively installed further and further into the hill, whilst the drainage had been improved with pumping and by clearing the bottom of the tunnel of the years of accumulated debris.

Both Americans were aware that the ore was not good, and knew that sooner or later it would have to be processed. They also knew that just about all the mining rights to the whole peninsula were owned by Japanese and American companies. Naturally enough, the illegality of their actions didn't worry them. There was enough of the lure of gold in me to understand exactly how they felt.

Boyd's part of the deal was to find out if nearby crushing was absolutely necessary, or if there'd be enough in it to make it worthwhile moving the raw ore to somewhere safe, where the job could be done without raising suspicion.

It turned out that Boyd's analysis was not required.

The old guy who was looking after the mine was found to be panning the drainage water with spectacular success — so much so that he had accumulated a worthwhile amount of dust in only two days' work.

This immediately altered the whole aspect of the operation of course. Boyd couldn't tell how long the dust would continue to run, but nobody really cared by then.

The Americans worked there on and off for most of the winter, making sure that their disappearances from civilisation were not too frequent. Boyd became responsible for slowly increasing the drainage into the mine and for advising on the design of the flume that had been built. During his weekends he supervised this and helped in the construction, occasionally taking days off in the week when he had time from his more mundane geological work.

Pretty soon, really substantial quantities of gold began to build up. Boyd, the Americans and the old man began to feel the real pull of the stuff.

I'd read about it, I could imagine it, and hearing Boyd's talking about the days in the hills I could sense the excitement that all of them must have felt.

Karen had remained impassive as she listened to her husband. When Boyd stopped for more beer I asked her, 'You knew what was going on?'

'More or less, Boyd wouldn't take me to the mine.'

Boyd said, 'It was part of the deal that it would only ever be the three or four of us if you count old Henry.'

'The old man?' I asked.

'Henry Galley — a real old miner.'

I said, 'It sounds as exciting as hell and just about as dangerous. How remote is the mine?'

Boyd grinned briefly. 'If I told you where it was you'd never find it — not even with a helicopter.'

'How'd you get supplies in?'

'On our bloody backs — literally

41

bloody sometimes.'

'So what happened after you all got gold fever?'

'We didn't — Henry did. Conway — one of the Americans — Charles Conway saw the old chap in Coromandel one Saturday — here in town I mean. He had five pounds of dust with him.'

'What happened?'

'Henry Galley fell under a car about half a mile from here on the same day.'

I whistled quietly, 'Your American friends sound a bit tough.'

Boyd passed his hand across his lips.

He said helplessly. 'Russ, so help me I don't know if it was an accident or not. The old man was pretty rocky and a raving alcoholic — the coroner's verdict was accidental death.'

'And the gold?'

'Conway brought it back to the mine — he said he took it from Henry over an hour before the accident took place.'

'And you believed him?'

'I did then.'

'What about now?'

'I guess not Russell — no not now.'

'What's the name of the other man?'

'Christopher Monroe.'

'So Mr. Conway and Mr. Monroe and Mr. Hallett carried on with their mine in the bush and forgot about poor Henry Galley?'

Boyd nodded. 'Yes, we carried on until about a month ago. Conway had to go back to the States and Monroe figured the risk was getting to be too high. I agreed with that so we all decided that the smart thing to do was to stop while we were winning. We intended to seal up the mine — just in case we needed it again — and then pull out.

'Although it sounds unbelievable, in less than six months we had extracted something like three hundred pounds of dust from a muddy stream of water coming out of a hole in the ground.'

'I stopped him, 'What's that worth?'

'I'm still not absolutely sure, but if you price gold at the current rate of thirty-one dollars per ounce you obtain the staggering figure of one hundred and fifty thousand dollars.'

Karen said quietly, 'Boyd's share was

fifty thousand dollars.'

I said, 'Wow,' astonished and at a loss for words.

My cigarette burnt my fingers. I lit another one.

'When did you close up?' I asked.

'Four weeks ago.'

'And where's the gold now?'

'It was in a hole in the ground about half a mile from the mine.'

'But it's not there now?'

'No.'

Things began to seem clearer. The time honoured double-cross had occurred.

I said, 'You'd better carry on and tell me the worst.'

He nodded.

'On September the first we were supposed to meet in Auckland to discuss the final arrangements for bringing the dust out of Coromandel. Conway and Monroe never showed up.

'Naturally, fearing the worst, I drove like hell up here on the same day — I had to leave a message for Karen because she was out somewhere — I can't remember where, anyway it doesn't matter.

'The weather was lousy, very wet and gloomy. I can still remember it well. I wasn't dressed for crawling around in the bush either. Before I reached the pit where we kept the dust I knew that they'd taken the lot. The wooden cover was lying on the ground.

'I had my old dog with me — old Crystal, you may remember her. She went up and sniffed in the hole. It was completely empty.

'Looking back now I suppose it's obvious that my partners were expecting me, seeing as they hadn't turned up for the meeting.

'The first I knew about it was when they shot Crystal — but she was okay and got away into the bush all right. I was scared half to death and started running. That's when I got this.'

Boyd pulled up his left trouser leg and rolled down his sock. On each side of his ankle were huge grotesque scabs of congealed blood. The leg was swollen and an ugly yellow colour.

'Gin trap,' I said.

Boyd grinned ruefully. 'They'd planted

the damn things all round the place. I trod right in the middle of one.

'But they didn't shoot you?' I asked.

'I've no idea why not, Russell — there was some shouting I heard before I passed out — that's all. The pain was pretty awful.'

I could imagine. I didn't even like looking at the puncture wounds that the cruel spikes had made in his leg.

Karen said, 'All I had was Boyd's note. When he didn't show up I phoned David and told him some of what was going on. He was mad and said to cable you at once. I didn't do it till later though.'

She smiled, 'I'm glad I did, but Russ why did I ever let him go in after Boyd?'

Boyd started talking again quickly. 'It took me nearly three weeks to get out. I knew what Karen must be thinking, I just had to hope she wouldn't do anything stupid. Most of the time I spent up at the mine where we had a bush shelter and some food. If that hadn't have been there I'd never have made it. I rested and waited for my leg to get well enough to walk on before I moved. By the time I finally reached civilisation David had already been found dead.'

'What happened to him exactly?' I asked.

'Nobody knows for sure, he was found hanging over a barbed wire fence shot through the head with his own rifle, about five miles inland from Otama beach.'

'That's in about the right area?'

'Near enough.'

And that seemed to be it. There was silence in the bedroom.

My watch said it was evening.

I said, 'You're staying tonight?'

Karen shook her head. 'Boyd and I have to go home to see my people in Wellington tomorrow — they couldn't get here for the funeral.'

'What about Conway, Monroe and the gold?' I had to ask.

'What about them Russ?' Karen said quietly.

I shut up. There was time to think about that. Or was there? They left almost at once. We arranged to meet the day after next at the Hallett's home in Howick, just south of Auckland city.

4

I didn't see the Halletts again before they left Coromandel.

My attempts at rational thought had been unsuccessful to say the least. There were too many questions rattling around inside my head that needed answers from Boyd. As well as that, I was still wondering about Karen and I.

There hadn't been time to analyse my feelings towards her. I realised that my reactions had been nothing other than those of an old friend — not that I was that old. It was something of a relief. To have experienced the old attraction, the intense closeness and the fondness would have been a bitter sweet thing to have come home to.

Just seeing her again had brought back the times of long ago as if recalling a dream on awakening. Karen was as lovely as ever, but I knew lots of lovely women. I suppose I felt as a brother feels towards a sister.

Boyd seemed a pretty right sort of guy. I even liked him. Certainly I couldn't call him a fool for what he'd done. I'd have done just the same, except that I might have been a bit more wary about the other guys.

I thought about David Wendle too.

I guess David had used his twenty-three years well, but twenty-three isn't many to have. A man has more to do than can be packed into a time that short.

There were a fair number of unexplainable events. Why had David been killed yet Boyd left alone whilst caught helpless in the trap? Why bother to kill either of them? All Conway and Monroe had to do was to take the dust and hightail.

Boyd would have the answers, or at least be able to guess at the answers to these questions. It was annoying not to be able to talk to him. My frustration nearly resulted in the purchase of another dozen cans of beer.

I went to bed early instead.

* ★ *

I awoke the next morning still haunted by the question which had kept me awake for part of the night.

Where was the gold now? Still in New Zealand? Did Boyd think there was still a chance of recovering his share and why couldn't we reopen the mine?

Although it doesn't sound like one question, it could be summed up simply by my realising that I was eager for Boyd to get his fifty thousand dollars. I had a nagging suspicion that I would like a share in the enterprise too.

My plan for today was to drive across to the east coast where, according to my map, I would find a road rejoicing in the name of Black Jack. That would get me as near to the Waitaia peak as the main road went. At least I'd be able to obtain some idea of the country in the vicinity of the mine. There was no point in trying to find it from what Boyd had said. Anyway there wasn't time and there could be no real purpose to it.

By the time I left the hotel the sun was

high. I had slept late. In case there were some nice open beaches I'd brought the rifle with me. Beaches are ideal for trying out new equipment, particularly because shooting into sand is very safe when you're using high velocity ammunition.

The little Volkswagen was willing. It's a good car for Coromandel driving. I was in no hurry today and I took my time to travel over the hills to the coast through the planted forests and the steep slopes of native bush. After about thirteen miles I knew I was near to Boyd's mine, close to where David had died. I didn't stop to explore but motored on directly to the coast.

At Opito Bay I turned, continuing until I found a long sweeping sandy beach. The tide was right in, the wind carrying the crash of the breaking waves across the sand to where I parked.

Carrying my rifle down the gentle slope to the shore, I was more than usually conscious of the colour of the sea, the texture of the sand and the wildness of the coast line.

Twelve shots were enough. The kick

against my shoulder and the sharp crack made me tingle with pleasure. I could see part of the beach exploding with puffs of sand near a large dune one hundred and fifty yards away.

I really tried with the last three. The final shot missed the piece of driftwood I was aiming at by less than two inches.

The old joy was in my bones. If I could have seen myself I'm sure I would be grinning like a fool.

I smoothed some streaks of oil along the slender barrel, cleaned the coarse grains of white sand from the stock and walked back to my car.

When I reached the Volkswagen I was mildly surprised to find a motionless bicyclist steadying himself by his boot which was planted squarely on the front bumper.

Two days back in New Zealand were enough to remind me of the accepted greeting in conditions such as this.

'I said, 'Gooday.'

'Weather's right now,' he answered without smiling.

He was about forty, dressed in a black

bush shirt, brown shorts and very substantial boots. As I was definitely cool in my sweater and jeans it was difficult to understand why he wasn't goose pimples all over. On the other hand, you would get very hot cycling in this part of the world. I thought that anybody using a bicycle on the Coromandel peninsula would either be extremely fit or possibly mad.

It seemed necessary to offer an explanation to account for my extraordinary behaviour.

'Just trying this out,' I waved the rifle at him.

He sat watching me as I packed my gear away in the car.

I hate making conversation, especially to complete strangers. Obviously he wanted something from me otherwise he would have removed his foot from the bumper and let me drive away.

'Haven't seen you before,' he stated.

'No, I'm on holiday — hunting.'

'You won't find much on the beach.'

'I wasn't hunting on the beach, I was practising.'

This was not going to be a pleasant chat in the morning sunshine. He appeared a truculent character. I wondered what he could want. On guard, I waited for the next question.

'Been here long?'

'No, I arrived from Canada yesterday.'

It was obviously an excellent answer. The boot was removed from my bumper.

Before he could move away I switched to the attack.

'You're after something, I have no idea what, but the fact that I'm a stranger round here seemed to make you hostile.'

'You really here to hunt?' he asked, still not sure.

'Pig.'

'Mate, you've got no show with an outfit like that — not with a little gun like that.'

'There must be other strangers around, why does it matter how long I've been here?' I ignored his caustic remarks about my hunting gear.

He looked at me trying to sum up his opinion of the curious Canadian with the little gun.

With gross disregard for the machine, he dropped the bicycle to the ground and sat on the coarse grass beside the road, indicating that I should do the same.

Before I joined him I opened the boot of the Volkswagen and withdrew my last two cans of beer. I hoped this long shot was going to be worth it.

He did something with the single brake lever on the handlebars of his bicycle and both cans were neatly open. My opinion of him rose.

'I've lived round here all my life, mate. I know everyone hereabouts and they all knows Jimmy Bleach.'

I offered my hand, 'Russ Gallagher.'

'How are you,' he said as he squashed my fingers.

After a long swig of beer he started talking.

'There used to be a lot of gold around here — still is if you know where to find it. I had a mate — old man Galley — lived about six mile from here. He knew where to find it.'

Suddenly I wished desperately I had

brought a bottle of whisky with me. Beer was not enough.

He continued, 'The old man died a few months back but he left enough for his missus so she'd be all right. Old Henry always had a bit about. Then last week some city jokers from Auckland turned up to talk to her. Next thing the cops is here, hills full of bloody people and a young joker's found dead in a sheep paddock.'

'What happened?' I tried not to appear too interested.

'Old Celia let on that her old man had been working in the hills over the winter and had left a bit of dust under the house. Stupid old sheila should've kept quiet but you know what them Government jokers is like.'

I nodded in sympathy.

'Anyway me brother was asked to help find out where old Henry was working — he's a good bushman. He said he wouldn't but the cops said he had to.'

'Didn't Mrs. Galley know?'

'If she did she wouldn't say — not after they took her gold. For her old age that was.'

'Have they found the — ' I nearly said mine 'place?'

'Yesterday morning.'

And Boyd told me the mine was virtually unfindable!

Jimmy Bleach's brother must be pretty damn good. I wondered if the police had connected David's death with the discovery of the mine.

I said, 'And you thought I was one of these city guys?'

He shook his head.

Suddenly I understood. Mr. Bleach had suspected me of being one of the people who'd been working the mine. He wasn't too far off either.

I grinned at him, 'I'm afraid I haven't been working up there but I could use some gold.'

'So could I — so could old Celia, mate.'

Cautiously I asked, 'Do they know who they are?'

He shrugged. 'Maybe they'll come back — either way they're in trouble, you can't unload dust in Coromandel or in Auckland neither.'

'How did Mr. Galley get on then?'

'Oh you can always sell a little over in Auckland or even around here if you know where, but no stranger's going to have a show of getting rid of a sugar bag full — 'specially not now.'

'Does anybody know how much they got out?'

'No, but me brother reckons they've been at it for some time.'

'This sort of thing go on very much over here?' I asked.

'First time I've heard of it being done big time. Mostly you've got to work like hell to get any dust at all — the ore's no good for it.'

'You don't think I should bother?'

That actually brought a half-smile to his face.

'You stick to playing with your popgun mate.'

I racked my brains for any other information that I could extract from my new friend.

'Did you say someone was found dead too?' Perhaps he had some news of David's tragic death.

'Young chap from Auckland — was in the paper.'

'Was he connected with the gold?'

'Don't know — doubt it — probably just after bunnies — just an accident.'

Mr. Bleach's hand crushed the empty beer can without apparent effort. He was going to leave.

Although reluctant to lose this valuable source of information, I had to be careful not to appear too interested even though I seemed to have been accepted as harmless.

He stood up and readied the bicycle.

There was a salute. 'Thanks for the beer mate — sorry if I was a bit sharp like — I hopes you get a good pig.'

Powered by the massive hairy legs of Mr. Bleach pumping up and down on the pedals, the bicycle moved away. There was something faintly ludicrous in the sight.

One thing was certain now. Neither Boyd nor his ex-American friends were going to get any more gold from their mine. Something was bothering me. I wasn't going to get any either.

5

On the return trip to Auckland on the following morning I took my time, allowing myself the luxury of being a tourist and stopping whenever I felt the need to enjoy a particularly beautiful strip of coastline.

My journey from Coromandel to the southern outskirts of Auckland city soon passed. I was certainly beginning to feel at home again.

Shortly after turning off the motorway, I noticed a small dairy some way down the road. It seemed to be an ideal opportunity to buy lunch.

Thirty minutes later I pulled up outside a small but well established weatherboard home overlooking Howick beach.

Boyd's blue Zephyr was in the driveway and Karen was cleaning squashed flies from the windscreen. She waved as I walked to the house.

The pinched look had disappeared but

she was still pale.

'Hi Russ,' she greeted me.

'How were your parents?'

She looked at the ground. 'About how I expected.'

She took my hand leading me up some concrete steps past a huge banana palm to the house.

Boyd stood up to meet me as Karen opened the big ranch sliders leading from the patio to the lounge. We shook hands.

Whilst he went to fetch the beer, Karen collected my suitcase from the car and I made a fuss of old Crystal. The wound in her back was healed, but she looked rather scruffy where the hair had been clipped back by the vet. I still couldn't understand why the Americans had tried to shoot her but had left Boyd alone.

When he returned I asked him again.

'I don't know Russ. I think the original idea might have been to kill both of us — Crystal could've got back without me and that would have started a search. All I can suggest is that they thought they'd got the dog but decided that I was sufficiently immobilised by the trap and didn't have to bother with a bullet. I don't think they would've wanted a murder on their hands if it could have been avoided.'

Karen had returned from the spare bedroom.

She said, 'Can't we talk about something else, please?'

I took a long drink from my glass.

I said, 'I have a proposition if you can call it that.'

Boyd said, 'No propositions.'

The statement was partially anticipated — I ignored it.

I said, 'I've thought a great deal about it and I can't see how any more harm can come to anybody except possibly me, and I think that's my business. The other thing is that I know exactly what I'm letting myself in for and anyway I have no one who's going to care about me one way or the other.'

Boyd said, 'No Russ, no!'

He really sounded as though he wanted me to stop.

Hurriedly I went on. 'My proposition is childishly simple — so simple that if you think I'm trying to make a fast buck you're dead right. In Canada I make a thousand dollars a month after tax — or when I'm working I do. Now I'm home I should like to act on your behalf, and with your help, to recover the portion of the dust that is rightfully yours or the cash equivalent which might be even better. If I succeed, you pay me for my time at the rate I mentioned, plus any expenses incurred along the way. If on the other hand I fail — you pay me nothing.'

Karen said, 'That's not fair.'

'Do you mean I'm being too greedy?'

'No — you know I didn't mean that. I mean that if you don't catch up with Conway and Monroe you'll be out of pocket on our behalf.'

I grinned at her, 'There's a catch though — two really. Firstly I have only a thousand dollars in round figures which I think will only get me on the trail and not much else — after that you're going to have to lend me the rest if it looks like it's going to be worth it. Secondly, if I get the dust back and not dollars, I should like to help you to sell it which is going to be rather tricky. For that I want ten per cent.'

Boyd was trying to look worried, unless he was worried — I couldn't tell which.

He said, 'If the stuff's already left the country there's no point at all in bringing it back in — New Zealand is the last place we want it to be.'

'Where should it go?' This was what I wanted to know.

'India or maybe France — that's one of the problems.'

I said, 'Well, what about it?'

'Why don't you want half or a third of it?' Boyd asked.

I didn't like the way he said it.

'Because I haven't done any work for it so far, and that's why if I supply you with cash I want no percentage.'

'Are you intending to get just my share back or all of it?' Boyd's manner had become slightly patronising.

'Do you figure you should have it all?'

'That's the way they figured it as you put it.'

'I think perhaps that's a question that can wait until we find Mr. Conway and

Mr. Monroe — maybe they'd like you to have it all.'

He laughed shortly. 'You'll never find them or the gold, Russell.'

'Suppose I do?'

'Then I'll pay your thousand a month.'

'And ten per cent for helping sell it?'

'Certainly.'

'So you agree to my proposition?'

'You're going to do it anyway, aren't you?'

'Yes, I am, Boyd.'

'Why?'

'Because I want to, because Karen's brother is dead and because I could use the money.'

Boyd said, 'So whether we want your help or not we still get it.'

He had stood up and was peering out across the lawn to the darkening sea. An uncomfortable silence filled the room.

I said, 'As you've agreed you can't really stop me, and as you've agreed to my terms, wouldn't it be better for all of us if we worked together? Besides, I need all the help and information I can get from you before I even start.'

Boyd said, 'I suppose you're right.' He didn't even turn round.

'Can we seal the deal on another beer?'

He wasn't pleased but there wasn't anything he could do about it. I wondered why I was pushing so hard.

Karen poured more beer for us. She didn't look as angry as her husband.

She said, 'Once Russ has made up his mind he won't budge Boyd — come on now — at least there's some chance of getting the gold back isn't there?

Boyd said, 'Russ isn't offering to do anything I couldn't do myself.'

I said quickly, 'But you have a wife and a home and job. I haven't any of those things.'

He said, 'I wish I'd never heard of gold — God I wish that so much!'

I said, 'I have to make a couple of calls this afternoon — if you'll invite me to dinner I'll be back at about six.'

Boyd recovered his poise. He said, 'Of course Russ — I'm sorry — it hasn't been easy lately as you can imagine.'

His anger appeared to have moderated. He looked dejected.

I finished the beer, said a quick, 'See you later' and walked lightly across the lawn to the Volkswagen.

When I was a mile down the road I stopped for a cigarette to unwind a bit and decide what to do with myself until six o'clock. I had no visits to make — I just thought it better to leave the Halletts alone for a few hours to talk to each other without me being there.

★ ★ ★

When I returned, Karen and Boyd were waiting in the lounge. Boyd appeared a lot less wary.

He said, 'It's okay Russ, the deal stands and sure you can help — it hurts to have lost out on so much. The only trouble is that I have just about nothing to go on I'm afraid.'

'You may know a whole lot more than you think — all we need is a lead — just one single lead. Anyway, sure as hell we'll give it a try.'

The Halletts' house is best described as comfortable without any claim to ostenta-tion, it had a lived-in look about it and wasn't particularly tidy.

We ate in a small dinette sandwiched between the lounge and the kitchen with lighted candles on the table although it wasn't dark enough for their effect to be felt properly.

Karen had changed from the jeans and blouse she had worn in the afternoon to a plain summer frock in a light yellow colour. She wore her long dark hair loose and looked very much like the Karen I remembered from the past. I could feel a small thing inside me wanting me to reach out and touch her.

Boyd sat with his broad back to the window, a solid chunk of a man with large facial features to fit. He made me feel small.

Suddenly I wondered if Boyd had derived some sort of pleasure in taking Karen away from me and if he felt that in some way he was the better man. The thought had never occurred to me before. I guess in that particular race he had indeed proved the winner.

When we had finished the trifle that Karen had made for dessert I became conscious of the need to prompt conversation.

To open the subject I pushed my chair back and issued an expectant, 'Well?'

After a brief silence Karen urged, 'Go on Boyd.'

He cleared his throat. 'I'm trying to think where to start — I suppose one thing we could do is write down everything I know about Conway and Monroe.'

Karen left the table for a moment and returned with a lined pad of foolscap and a ball-point pen.

'Where were they staying here in Auckland?' I asked.

Boyd said, 'I think they started off in the Intercontinental Hotel in town when they first came down from the north, but after that they moved to a motel at Eastern Beach just up the coast from here.'

'When did they check out?' I asked.

'A week before I got back to Coromandel — I phoned this afternoon and asked. No forwarding address of course.'

'Does the Intercontinental or the motel

have their U.S. address?'

Boyd laughed shortly. 'Yes, they both do. Seattle, Washington, U.S.A.'

I thought for a moment. There was just a chance, a tiny slender chance.

Before I could speak Karen said, 'There's only one other place they know really.'

I said, 'Go on, it's my money, start phoning all the motels and hotels in the Bay of Islands area. There's an N.Z. travel book in my car.'

'You're wasting your time,' Boyd was very sarcastic. 'Why on earth should they go back there?'

'Because they're in a strange land and it's a place they know and one where they may even have friends.'

Soon, Karen could be heard asking for tolls on the phone in the lounge. She had fetched the book and had started right away. I hoped this was going to be one of the better Gallagher long shots.

Boyd and I talked about his ex-partners until I had built a reasonable mental picture of them. I thought Boyd was an odd sort of guy in some ways, he didn't seem after their blood or his share of the gold.

From the other room Karen's voice sounded brightly as she contacted hotel after hotel. If my notion was going to have proved correct, I thought that she should have hit pay dirt by now. Boyd seemed to feel the same.

He said, 'Karen's wasting her time, Russ.'

I stood up nodding to him. It was a stupid idea. I walked to the lounge to stop her before she spent all my first month's money.

As I reached the door there was a joyful shriek, a bang as the receiver was slammed down and Mrs. Hallett was leaping up and down on the thick pile carpet.

When she stopped she handed me a crumpled slip of paper.

It read, 'Marlin Motel, Kerikeri.'

'They're there?' I asked.

'Both of them — you were right, you were right, you were darned well right.'

She was bright eyed and very breath-less.

Visibly shaken and by no means as elated as his wife, Boyd just couldn't believe it.

I said, 'Then I can start work can't I?'

The Halletts looked at me, Karen smiling and her husband nodding slowly.

Until well past midnight that evening, we talked. I went to bed in a state of considerable excitement wondering what I had let myself in for.

Plans had been made for me to leave for the north first thing in the morning.

6

My heart was beating so quickly that the blood pulsing in my ear made a low roar as I pressed the side of my head hard against the wall. After a few minutes the ear was painful and very hot. I couldn't hear anything, which meant either that they weren't talking or that the acoustics were worse than I had anticipated.

I crept away from the wall and lay down on the single bed, placed unimaginatively in the centre of the small motel room. It was very quiet, although earlier, now and again, there had been a faint squeak from the floor boards.

The motel was arranged in two identical blocks, each containing three room units. Only one of the blocks was in use at this time of year, and I had been fortunate enough to be able to check into the remaining empty room — the centre one of course, because any thinking guest would automatically choose accommodation on an outer wall.

I hadn't asked if a Mr. Conway and a Mr. Monroe were staying here. Karen's phone call was suspicious enough without me arriving later asking the same question.

Two hours after sunset the Americans had returned to the motel. Recognition had not been difficult; the description Boyd had given me was excellent. Conway, I knew, was the short stocky man and Monroe the one with the slight stoop.

Although the lights in the parking area of the motel had not been bright enough to allow a really good look, and to aggravate matters they had parked their car in the shadow of one of the disused blocks, I had still been able to watch them for a good ten or fifteen seconds — the time it took them to walk from the car to the door of their motel room.

From then until midnight I had heard nothing from next door, and it soon became obvious that everybody was asleep except me.

After the long drive from Auckland my body felt tired and listless from hours of sitting in the driving seat. It meant I should try and get some exercise if I was to be fresh for the morning.

I thought that I should go for a walk to try for inspiration — I hadn't locked up the Volkswagen either.

In the end I thought about it too long. I had sufficient energy to find my pyjama trousers, crawl between the starched sheets of the bed and that was all.

The last thing I can remember was thinking that even though winter was coming, it would've been better to be back in Montreal in my own room with a known tomorrow to look forward to.

★   ★   ★

I have no idea how long I'd been asleep when I heard the noise. Under normal circumstances I am one of those people who can sleep through a thunderstorm — if I ever wake up in the middle of the night I immediately start worrying what's wrong with me. But this time I was glad that I had woken. I was sure somebody was in the room.

Regulating my breathing to what I hoped was the same frequency as it had been when I was asleep, I slowly opened an eye. Luckily I was lying facing the window and could see the glow of the outside lights through the small gap I had made between two slats of the blinds. No sooner had I picked up this reference point than it vanished. Someone was either inside or outside my room, moving quietly in front of the light.

Utterly terrified, I reacted immediately. In one swift movement I drew my legs up to my chest, pushed myself from the covers and landed heavily on the floor behind the bed.

A dark shape moved silently towards me from the window.

Violently I hurled myself across the bed aiming my hands for the throat of the intruder. I never made contact.

Half-way to my target something crashed into the centre of my back creating a pain so intense and so paralysing that it was a merciful relief to slip into unconsciousness.

★ ★ ★

When I came to, I would have given all the money I've ever had to be unconscious again, but my brain wouldn't allow it. Why the hell my body thought it was better off in a conscious state I couldn't imagine. The entire length of my backbone felt smashed and the pain of it was awful.

Two men — my neighbours from next door, were sitting in the white wooden motel chairs. A pillow case was tied over the lampshade, allowing only a dim light to fill the room.

I was lying on my back on the bed with my wrists tied above my head to the frame of the bed. My ankles were tied together too.

In waves now, starting from my shoulder blades and sweeping down to my pelvis, pain racked my body.

When a brief period of respite allowed me to think of something other than the agony, I said, 'For God's sake untie me, I think my back's broken.' It sounded like a whine.

The shorter man, Conway, left his chair and began to fumble with the nylon ropes. He didn't look at me.

As soon as my hands were free I moved my arms gratefully down to my sides. Surprisingly the relief was immediate, my spine felt a lot less painful.

The American said, 'Turn over — let me see.'

He had a deep voice sounding more familiar to my Canadian senses than the Kiwi accent I had been hearing for the past few days.

I could feel his fingers probing my backbone. There was no additional pain, just a dreadful numbness all over.

'You'll be okay,' he said gruffly. 'Just one big bruise about three feet long.'

I turned slowly on to my stomach again. The stabbing, smashed feeling had abated significantly.

I said, 'What the hell did you hit me with?'

The other man, who had remained

seated, raised something slightly.

'This,' he said.

It was my rifle and it was pointed at my crotch.

'You were lucky, you were supposed to get it across the back of your head.' He grinned artificially from a coarse-featured face.

My sudden spring forward across the bed must have caused the man behind me to miss. Building up energy, the rifle stock had crashed down onto my back. I cursed for not realising that there would be two of them.

I said, 'Who are you, and what the hell are you doing breaking into my room in the middle of the night?'

Trying to sound indignant was impossible — I hurt too much.

Conway had returned to his chair. He lit a cigarette.

I fumbled for mine in the drawer beside the bed. For once the effect of the smoke was detectable, I drew hungrily on the paper tube.

Monroe said, 'Are you from the United States, Mr. Gallagher?'

How did they know my name? My mind raced furiously.

I said, 'I demand an explanation, or perhaps the police would be better at demanding, my back hurts like hell. What do you want?'

'No, I don't think you are an American,' Monroe spoke again.

Conway said, 'It's more a question of what you want don't you think?'

'I don't know what you mean.'

Conway looked pained. He stubbed out his cigarette and stared pointedly at me. He said, 'Look buddy, we're not going to get anywhere if you're going to be dumb. Someone telephoned this motel last night asking if we were staying here — the old lady in reception told us this morning. You arrive the next day. So we took a little look in your car when everyone had gone to sleep.'

He reached into the pocket of his jeans, producing a crumpled piece of blue paper. I recognised it at once. It had been in the glove box of the VW; my bill from the hotel at Coromandel.

Conway was speaking again.

'One side of this bit of paper has 583 Marine Parade, Howick written on it and the other has the address of this motel.'

I interrupted him, 'So that allows you to force the door of my room and beat me up with a rifle butt does it?' I realised I was feeling a little better.

Conway ignored the remark.

'What does Boyd want?' he asked.

It seemed pointless to continue with what was obviously a stupid bluff on my part.

I said, 'What the hell do you think he wants!'

This time it was Monroe who replied. He was still holding my rifle.

He said, 'That's better, now perhaps we can talk intelligently.'

I answered him angrily, 'If all you wanted was a talk why the rough stuff?'

'Mr. Gallagher,' he said sarcastically. 'We were just having a quiet look round your room to see what we could find — you started the fight.'

Monroe was an unpleasant looking man. He had thick lips that are characteristic of some North Americans.

His skin was oily with big open pores and thick black hair fell untidily over his forehead.

I didn't like the way he kept moving the muzzle of the Marlin, first to the top of my body and then back to my feet.

Conway said, 'Are you working with Hallett?'

'No,' I said, hoping I could back up my choice of answer.

'But you know what he wants?'

'Of course, his share of the dust.'

Conway smiled. He turned to his companion.

'Mr. Gallagher thinks Boyd wants his share of the dust.'

Monroe flicked at the safety catch of the rifle with a fingernail.

He said, 'We seem to be talking at cross purposes.'

'And what do you want Mr. Gallagher?' Conway asked.

I had my answer ready. I prayed it would work.

I said, 'I want ten per cent to move it for you.'

There was a moment's silence. Eventually Monroe stood up placing the Marlin in the corner of the room.

He said, 'You know about the gold and about David Wendle?'

'I know you killed him.' I hoped it wasn't stupid admitting I knew about David's death. After all, as far as I knew, Conway and Monroe probably had killed him.

Conway said, 'It was an accident — he was stupid.'

So that was the end of that. They had murdered David. I could feel the hate well up inside me.

He said, 'And you want ten per cent?'

'To help you sell it — I have contacts.'

'And if we don't want to take advantage of your offer, then you'll go to the police about the boy?'

'I've made no decision one way or the other about that yet.'

Monroe approached the bed. He pushed my feet to one side and sat down.

He said, 'Let's get this straight, Gallagher. Somehow or other you've stumbled on our little enterprise over on the peninsula and discovered Boyd Hallett's address in Auckland. You've approached him with an offer to sell the gold and he's told you that he hasn't got it . . . So you poke around until you find us here in Kerikeri and are now making us the same offer.'

I said. 'Right, I can unload twenty pounds a week at the full price for you with virtually no risk.'

Both Americans were looking thoughtful.

My bluff seemed to have been accepted and, from the rate that the feeling was returning to my spine, I figured that perhaps it was only badly bruised. The situation was improving.

There was no longer a gun on me either, reinforcing my belief that my story had been swallowed.

Conway said, 'Suppose we've sold it already?'

'Then five thousand dollars to me isn't going to hurt you and I'll guarantee to keep quiet about David Wendle.'

He said, 'Mr. Gallagher, we have some bad news for you. You've been had. We haven't got the gold — Hallett stole it all.'

'But — '

A cold tingle of fear crept into my stomach.

Conway continued. 'Hallett took it all from the hiding place at the mine and set traps all round. We caught him at it and had a shoot out right there in the woods. Somehow or other he got away. We spent days trying to find him until the boy disturbed us one night. We guessed he was working with Hallett and tried to make him take us to him, but he wouldn't. The young fool tried to escape one afternoon and Monroe shot him. We fixed his body so it looked like an accident and came up here to think. I can assure you we don't have the gold, but I can guarantee that we're not going to leave New Zealand without it.'

I couldn't believe it. Conway had to be lying — but why should he? Boyd had the gold all the time! I'd been played for a complete sucker. God, what had I become mixed up with? Did Karen know?

Perspiration ran in cold rivulets from beneath my arms.

Monroe said, 'You look worried, Gallagher.'

He leant forward, 'You should have stayed in Auckland, shouldn't you?'

His big hands caught my wrists and held them.

Conway produced some cord from the floor and systematically tied my limbs together. My struggles were ineffective. I was still weak and both Americans were strong men.

A face cloth was forced into my mouth and I was lifted off the bed.

Cautiously Monroe opened the door of the room and took a brief look outside.

Conway, the short man, carried me to the Chrysler in the car park and stood waiting while Monroe opened the boot.

I was thrown roughly in, gasping in pain as my injured back twisted over the hard steel edge.

The lid slammed, leaving me in utter darkness.

7

For what I judged was the remainder of the night I lay in the cramped confines of the steel box, trying in vain to free my wrists from the coarse stranded nylon. Initially I was able to breathe through my nose, but as the air became stuffier it became increasingly difficult.

Soon it was a real effort to obtain enough oxygen through my blocked nasal passages, and I realised that unless I could somehow pull the ball of material from my swollen mouth I was finished.

Whilst I tried to grip the protruding end of the gag between my knees, my tortured mind tried to grasp the fact that Boyd had lied to me. It was difficult to decide how much of what he had told me had been the truth. The wound in his ankle was real enough and there were numerous other points which quite obviously couldn't be lies. No wonder he hadn't been enthusiastic about my offers to help — I must have fouled everything up for him.

I imagined that he was expecting Conway and Monroe to come after him sooner or later. Perhaps he intended to use the murder of his brother-in-law to keep them quiet. Karen, I was sure, was as ignorant of the truth as I.

Then suddenly, at long last, I succeeded in snagging the corner of the facecloth on what I thought must be part of the boot lid catch mechanism. With infinite care, my injured back screaming in protest, I moved my head away, pushing on the fabric with my tongue. Just before I was able to take my first wonderful gulp of stale fetid air, the doors of the car opened and banged shut.

Immediately the engine started, exhaust fumes filled the boot compartment causing another wave of panic to seize me. Was I to be gassed now I had removed the gag?

I should have realised that the fumes would disappear when the car started moving, but I was well past coherent thought by the time forward motion started to provide a welcome draught of cool air through the seal of the boot lid.

Still dressed only in my pyjama trousers I began to chill. Quite obviously I had been in no real danger of asphyxiation — there were leaks everywhere. Streams of cold air poured in from the floor, the sides and the lid.

Apart from a single stop for about ten minutes, ending with a clanking noise on the floor when the driver returned, the speed of the car remained quite constant.

Then, after what I judged was a couple of hours, the car turned onto an unsealed road. The ride in the boot became extremely harsh whilst choking dust swirled in the air. I can remember thinking somewhat foolishly that I would never buy a Chrysler if the boot compartments were all like this one.

When eventually we stopped, I eagerly anticipated the lifting of the lid, allowing me to stretch my limbs and ease my tortured spine.

I could hear them talking but the voices were receding.

I was to be left in the boot.

Reason deserted me for a moment. Uncoiling my body I kicked and hammered with hands and feet on the hard metal. I shouted at the top of my voice.

Suddenly there was a click and daylight flooded my prison causing me to squint painfully. Hands lifted me out and I felt the blessed warmth of the morning sun on my naked chest.

'Don't you like it in there?' It was Monroe.

My hands and wrists were bloody where I'd tried to free myself. Fine yellow dust covered my body, stuck in a random pattern to the streaks of sweat. I was too exhausted to answer him.

'Up there,' he pointed to a crude trail leading from the track where the car was parked. He untied me roughly.

Stumbling more than walking I followed the two men up the steep eroded clay path. They seemed to naturally assume I would not attempt to escape and they were right. I was in no fit state to do anything other than seek food, water, and a place where I could lie down with my legs outstretched. For some inexplicable reason I believed these simple needs would be satisfied at the end of the path now winding its way through a dense stand of indigenous bush.

After a hundred yards, a sharp turn to the left round a mature king fern brought the trail out into a clearing. A tiny white weatherboard shack with a huge sundeck stood on four massive pine log pillars, rather like the pictures I've seen of houses built in swamps in other parts of the world.

Wooden steps led to the sundeck and then suddenly I could see why someone had taken the time and trouble to build in such a place. The view was stupendous.

Even in my physical condition, I couldn't help but stare at the ocean laid out in front of the little house.

Promontories lined each side of the bay below, both tapering gracefully into the sea, ending in a chain of varying sized rocks standing sentry-like, guarding the entrance to a small sandy beach. There was no sign of any other habitation whatever.

'Great, isn't it?' Conway asked.

I nodded. 'I need a drink,' I said.

'Help yourself.' He was less curt than Monroe in his address.

I discovered a tiny kitchen with a perished rubber tube tied back on itself hanging over a sink. Rusty water poured from the tube when I undid the knots. When it ran a little clearer I let some trickle into my mouth, feeling it soothe my swollen tongue and gums.

Conway had come in from the sundeck to prepare a meal. He produced three enamelled plates from a drawer and started opening cans.

In a few minutes I was sitting in the sunshine with my captors, eating corned beef and tinned pears. Soon I began to feel human again, things weren't so bad after all.

Conway gave me a cigarette.

Monroe was standing with his back against the house, staring through a very large pair of binoculars.

He lowered them slowly and said, 'We have decided that for the time being you will stay here while we go back to Auckland to see our old friend Boyd.'

I said, 'I have a feeling you won't find him there.'

Conway answered easily. 'You might be right but we think we won't have too much trouble finding Mrs. Hallett. She'll do.'

It seemed a pretty obvious method of bringing Boyd to heel, but I winced inwardly at the thought of Karen being mixed up in this again, especially as a hostage.

I said, 'Maybe one hundred and fifty thousand dollars is worth more to Boyd Hallett than his wife.'

Monroe said, 'I doubt it, but we'll see.'

'Then what?' I asked.

'Then either we get the gold out in the way that we originally thought of or you sell it for us.'

'For ten per cent?'

'For sweet nothing, buddy!'

'I won't be able to arrange it from here.'

'Nobody expects you to.'

'And afterwards?'

'You're an accomplice to the whole deal including the killing of the boy

— you'll keep quiet and you'll do it.'

So I was accepted as someone who could sell the gold for them and they had no intention of killing me. I experienced a wave of relief — at least there was time now.

'How are you going to keep me here?' I enquired.

Conway answered, 'Easy, so easy you'll never believe it.'

Monroe said, 'I'll get it.'

He returned shortly, carrying with difficulty a large quantity of iron chain, the kind used for anchoring small yachts.

'You might like to put on some pants before we fix you up,' Monroe grinned, handing me my old suitcase. He had brought it up from the car with the chain. 'We paid your motel bill too.'

Conway looped the chain four times round my ankle before snapping the loose end to another link with a very large steel padlock. Monroe carried the other end down the steps, fastening it with another padlock to the wheel of an old rusty grass cutter, the type used behind a tractor for cutting hay. It looked very solid and quite immovable.

I inspected a link of the chain.

Conway said, 'If you had a hacksaw — no problem but with a can opener or your teeth no chance at all.'

I said, 'How long will you be?'

He shrugged. 'No idea, but you'll still be here when we get back.'

Monroe was shouting something from the ground.

Conway said, 'See you later and don't get lost in the bush.'

He ran heavily down the steps to join his companion.

Minutes later I heard the car start and listened to the receding noise of its exhaust as it moved off along the bumpy coastal track. Soon the surf became dominant and I realised that I was quite alone somewhere in the north of New Zealand, chained like an animal to an ancient agricultural implement.

In recognition of my total failure, with my fetters carefully arranged beside me, I lay full length on the deck and went to sleep with the sun warm on my poor bruised back.

★ ★ ★

It was late afternoon when I awoke. I felt refreshed, slightly sunburnt and very stiff.

When I moved, the chain rattled annoyingly but I had several ideas about how to fix that. Obviously the cottage must be situated in an extremely remote spot, otherwise I wouldn't have been left here. I figured therefore that my chances of attracting attention were probably nil. Of course I could set fire to the bush but that seemed unnecessarily drastic — anyway it was just as likely to backfire — literally — and burn down the cottage with me in it. There was an easier way and the sooner I got started the better.

Like an old ghost, I clanked around inside the little house until I found what I was searching for. Then I started collecting wood from the grassy clearing. My chain gave me a working radius of thirty feet from the grass cutter and by nightfall, if there was a single piece of combustible material left in a circle of that size I would have been most surprised.

As the weather was fine it seemed sensible to begin straight away. In New Zealand it is always possible that it may rain tomorrow or even in the next half-hour. However, the weather appeared quite settled so I lit my fire.

When it was going well, and charcoal began to accumulate in a glowing layer on the ground, I carefully laid a part of my chain on a particularly hot section. Although I wanted to sever the links as closely as possible to my ankle, in fact the nearest I could hold my leg to the flames was about three feet, and then only by sheltering behind an old sheet of corrugated iron.

Working almost continuously from behind my shield, I built a fierce fire around the chain, lifting the links onto an ever increasing thickness of white hot charcoal.

When at last there was a foot of chain at the same temperature as the fire I dragged it quickly onto a flat slab of stone. Then, placing the blade of the screw driver I had found in the house, squarely on the nearest hot link, I began pounding with a chunk of grey rock picked up during my search for wood.

After a dozen bangs, the link cooled too much and the screwdriver was too hot to hold. I returned the chain to the fire, noting with gratification the deep vee nearly one third of the way through the steel link.

In fact it took six separate heatings altogether. Towards the end my screwdriver became rather blunt and it proved more difficult to expand the severed link than I had expected.

But no matter, I was a free man again — or at least a free man with three feet of chain round his leg. I thought three feet was a lot better than thirty feet and a grass cutter.

For the rest of the night I lay uncomfortably on one of the two bunk beds in the living area of the cottage whilst I tried to decide on my best course of action. There was only one really sensible thing to do — go back to Canada and forget that anything had happened, but I knew I couldn't do that now Karen was in danger.

My previous sleep in the afternoon prevented anything more than fitful dreaming until daybreak. It was a relief to my back to climb out of the primitive canvas bed to watch the sun rise out of the Pacific, illuminating the little bay with the first clear rays of morning.

I was sure that I could easily walk down the road until I found civilisation. Then, with a map, I could determine where the cottage was so that I could arrange a dramatic rescue of Karen if they brought her back here. There was doubt in my mind that they would bother to kidnap her and drive all the way back up to Kerikeri. It would be much easier to negotiate from Auckland.

There was an even chance that I could prevent the kidnapping from taking place. It all depended on how fast Conway and Monroe intended to move.

After a substantial canned breakfast, I wrapped my chain securely around my calf over an old shirt, pulled down my trouser leg and set off purposefully to the nearest town wherever it might be.

Four hours walking brought me to

larger road where a local farmer picked me up in his old station wagon and informed me that I was at Whangaruru North. I didn't like to tell him I was no wiser for the advice. He drove me about ten miles up the road and dropped me outside a small general store.

From there I hitched a ride with a surf fisherman in a rather nice Ford all the way to Russell.

I caught the ferry there and then, two buses later, I was back in Kerikeri. It was late afternoon before I had the Volkswagen burning up the miles to Auckland, the chain still heavy on my leg.

Unused on the seat beside me was a new hacksaw and a whole packet of blades.

8

Even in the dark I knew the house was empty. Milk bottles stood cold and pale by the mail box at the gate, and morning and evening newspapers, rolled in their brown paper wrappers, lay on the driveway near the road.

I told myself that this was what I had expected, I'd been telling myself for the last hundred miles. There was still the twinge of disappointment though, and the knot of fear for Karen was still in my stomach.

Parking the car in the drive, I walked up the steps to the big sliding windows of the lounge. A massive flake of glass lay on the concrete where the exterior handle had been wrenched off and there was a gap between the two sliding panels big enough for a man to walk through.

Now I was more worried. Had Conway and Monroe broken in after the Halletts had left — or before? Had they forced their way into the house to kidnap Karen whilst Boyd was away? — I had no way of knowing.

With some hesitation I walked into the lounge and switched on the light. Everything looked as it had done when I had been here last, in fact it looked so similar that I started to wonder if the Halletts had left at the same time that I had.

In the kitchen, the washing-up had all been done so Karen must have been home for at least some of the time. There was no reason for her to have left unless Boyd had decided to explain everything. He must have known I would be back sooner or later to ask him why he had lied about the gold.

As I saw the situation there were two choices open to him; either take off, leaving Karen to face me — or to tell her the truth and to persuade her that I would only stir up a hornet's nest; in which case it would be better for them to leave Howick at least for a while.

From the general appearance of the rooms I would have said that no extensive preparations for a prolonged absence had been made. There were suits and dresses in the bedroom wardrobes and the bathroom even contained a half-used tube of toothpaste, although both toothbrushes were missing from the plastic cup beside the handbasin.

My personal length of chain was still in the car. Stopping just south of Whangarei for a call of nature on the drive back, I had taken the opportunity to quickly saw through the clasp on the padlock. It was much easier than belting a blunt screwdriver through a red hot steel link.

Physically I was in poor shape, mainly from lack of proper sleep. How much of the pain in my back was due to the bruise alone was impossible to tell, there hadn't been one single real opportunity to rest it since the rifle stock had smashed into me. At the cottage I had managed to sleep a little but not in a conventional bed; the double bed in the Halletts' home began to look increasingly inviting.

The urge to keep after the Americans and to find Karen made me fidgety. Smoking I walked aimlessly from one room to another trying to think of some positive move I could make — but soon became conscious that my initiative was not up to the standard of the characters you read about in paperback novels.

The refrigerator provided a solitary can of beer on which to feed my grey matter, but, as I feared, it was not enough; if there had been a crate in the house I'm sure I could have done better.

Two hours later I was in the Halletts' bed with one slender idea. In the morning I would phone my way through those yellow pages advertising kennels in an attempt to find Crystal and the temporary address of her owner.

*　*　*

The idea seemed less attractive in the light of the morning; I knew there was only a slim chance that the dog had been boarded out but, perhaps because of her recent wound, Boyd hadn't taken her with him.

My depression was caused by the rain I told myself. Until today there hadn't been a break in the weather during the short time I'd been home but nevertheless the miserable drizzle outside was obviously a bad omen.

A modest breakfast of toast and coffee cheered me up enough to start telephoning. I remembered that my long shot of phoning the motels in the Bay of Islands had paid off — maybe my luck would hold.

There were only nine kennels listed — it was pitifully few. I started with the last one, introducing myself as Mr. Hallett's brother and explaining that I understood Crystal was being boarded there. Not only did the technique work badly — the lady on the other end became confused — but they had no dog there by that name.

Next, for no reason whatever, I chose the Hacienda Kennels at Whitford. Whitford, I recalled whilst dialling the number was not far from Howick — an obvious choice after all.

'Oh, good morning,' I said. 'Could you tell me if you have a dog called Crystal staying with you — the owner's name is Hallett.'

There was the slightest pause. 'Yes we do.' The educated feminine voice answered brightly.

'I wonder if you have Mr. Hallett's temporary address please, I'm trying to get hold of him rather urgently.'

'One moment sir.'

It had worked! I was unreasonably pleased with my cleverness.

After thanking the woman, I wrote down the address.

Waihi Hotel — presumably at Waihi, the town near the east coast just south of the Coromandel peninsula. My guide book confirmed that the Waihi Hotel was indeed where it should be; I could be there in a couple of hours — maybe three.

Fighting down the urge to telephone the hotel, remembering the result of Karen's phone call to the Kerikeri motel, I carefully destroyed the piece of paper I had just written on. I was learning fast.

In Howick I cashed a hundred dollar traveller's cheque, filled my rental car with gas and was on my way back to Coromandel by nine-thirty.

The trip to Waihi was made up by the major portion of the route that I had taken to Thames on the day I'd arrived in the country, plus a section leading south through a little town called Paeroa. About half way there the rain stopped. I enjoyed the drive, although by now I was beginning to wish I had rented a more powerful and a rather more comfortable vehicle.

Shortly after leaving Paeroa the road passed through a gorge becoming so narrow and winding that I used third gear for mile after mile wondering how long I would have to endure the twists.

It was just past midday when I drove casually past the revolving door of the Waihi Hotel trying to make the Volkswagen appear more unobtrusive than usual. I parked on the main street, on the same side of the road as the hotel about a hundred yards further up the slight hill.

Walking back, I kept as close as possible to the shop fronts — just in case Karen or Boyd were looking out of a bedroom window. Not that it was likely at this time of day, but I wanted there to be no chance of Boyd taking off before I talked to him. Finding him again would not be so easy.

On the way here I had tried to decide what Boyd was doing in Waihi but had been unable to think of one good reason. Either he was hiding or there was some scheme for disposing of the dust that required him to be here. I couldn't even be sure that Karen was with him.

The receptionist was not unlike a small railway porter.

'Mr. Hallett is expecting me — my name is Gallagher,' I said to him.

His eyes barely left the racing page, open on the counter in front of him.

'Room four, third floor,' he muttered.

Either there was no phone to the room or he considered that my visit was not sufficiently important to bother.

Walking across the dim foyer to the wide carpeted stairs my peripheral vision picked up the movement of the revolving door at the entrance. Turning my head slightly with natural curiosity I saw a tall man walking to the desk.

It was Monroe.

I swore under my breath. Damn them — how the hell had they found out the Halletts were here?

Monroe hadn't seen me, of that I was certain. After all, I was probably the last person he expected to find in Waihi.

There were only seconds before he would start following me up the stairs. I had to find room four before he did.

Taking two stairs at a time, I consumed three flights very quickly, although my legs and back barely stood the strain.

Room four was to the right of the landing. I banged on the door using a suitably urgent frequency, hoping desperately that someone was inside.

I heard Karen say, 'Come in.'

Monroe would be starting on the second flight of stairs by now.

I burst into the room, pushed the door quickly shut, turned the key and grinned at an astonished Karen who was staring at me open mouthed in amazement.

She was going to speak and Monroe would already be within thirty feet.

Walking to her with a finger on my lips I put my hand softly over her mouth. I motioned with my free hand for us to sit down on the bed.

Wide-eyed, Karen looked frightened now.

There was a heavy knock on the door.

I kept my hand over her mouth, not being able to avoid sensing the moistness and softness of her lips.

Monroe said, 'Mr. Hallett.' It didn't sound like him.

The door handle turned but there was no real pressure exerted on the lock.

I gave him time to decide that the room was unoccupied and start his walk back down the stairs.

Quietly I said, 'Where's Boyd?'

Karen shook her head, she was white. 'He said he'd be back for dinner tonight — Russ what's — ?'

I stopped her. 'No questions, there isn't time — we have about fifty seconds before Monroe comes back. The receptionist knows you're here and I gave him my name.'

'Monroe!'

I moved to the window. Outside in the street, Conway was sitting in the Chrysler close to the hotel entrance.

'Karen, is Boyd's car here?'

'Yes, he left me the key — here,' she passed it to me.

I gave it back to her and pulled her to the window.

'Over there — that corner,' I pointed.

'Yes?'

'You are to get Boyd's car and pick me up there — keep the engine running.'

She nodded.

I said, 'Good girl,' and squeezed her shoulders.

Suddenly, a series of knocks rattled on the door.

Monroe said, 'Mrs. Hallett?'

Perhaps the receptionist hadn't mentioned that I'd preceded Monroe up the stairs after all.

Gently I pulled Karen to the wall adjacent to the door.

Putting my mouth close to her ear, I said, 'When I say go — go. I'll see you at the corner.'

With one quick motion I unlocked the door, wrenching it open as fast as it would swing. Monroe stood there somewhat stupidly.

111

Using both hands with all the force I could muster I hit him in the stomach. As he began to fold and his head came forward I brought my knee up hard into his face.

Blood pouring from his nose, he staggered into the room.

'Go Karen,' I shouted.

She slipped behind me, running lightly down the stairs, leaving me to close the door and lock it from the outside. The damned key wouldn't even penetrate the crude wooden keyhole — I left it and ran.

There was no sign of her by the time I walked across the foyer and out onto the sidewalk. I thought perhaps there was a rear door to the hotel car park.

Using my handkerchief to cover my face, as if blowing my nose, I walked behind the rear of the Chrysler towards my car.

I saw the blue Zephyr sneak round the corner, its exhaust puffing from too much choke.

As usual the VW started at once. I waited until the road was clear in both directions and then pulled out into a direct U turn, accelerating down the hill towards the hotel. Just before drawing level with the Chrysler I opened my door and swung the steering wheel violently to the right.

The 'beetle' swerved obediently and with a deafening crash piled into the larger car just forward of the driver's door.

Conway's startled face showed at the window just before impact. He was lucky I'd hit where I had aimed and not further back.

Then I was out of the Volkswagen running to the Zephyr.

Karen had the door open ready for me, and the car was already moving when I dived in.

'Where to?' she shouted.

I grinned at her as she slammed into second gear.

'Anywhere,' I said. 'Anywhere at all.'

9

Seven roads led out of Waihi, three of which could be classed as arterial routes although on the peninsula the term is hardly appropriate. The map I found in the glove compartment showed that all the others eventually disappeared to nothing deep in the hills. I wondered which one we were on.

Karen seemed to have become inspired by the violent events preceding our flight. For brief periods, with engine working hard, the car accelerated and then suddenly we would be entering another curve, the tyres howling in agony and Karen fighting the wheel until we were in top gear again.

I endured it for three or four miles whilst I tried to collect my thoughts. Then I realised that we were heading back to Paeroa on the road I had travelled earlier in the day. I remembered the twisting through the gorge too.

'It's all right Karen — easy,' I made a slowing motion with my hand.

She let the car decelerate slowly from its headlong rush — it took some time before there was any noticeable reduction in speed.

When at last we were travelling at a rate more in keeping with road conditions, I lit a cigarette, put the map away in the glove box and turned to explain my behaviour to Karen.

Before I could begin she started firing questions at me.

'Russ, why did you hit that man — Monroe. And then crashing your car like that — you could have killed the driver — what on earth's going on — I don't understand and — ?'

I stopped her, realising that I'd better ask some questions of my own first.

'What was Boyd doing in Waihi?' I asked.

'I don't know.'

'He must have said something.'

'Only that it was important we both came down here.'

'Didn't you ask why?'

'No, not really. Boyd has been pretty funny since David's funeral — he gets very angry if I ask him about things too much — you've seen what he's like. I did say I wanted to know why we had to go to Waihi before we left home but he started to get mad so I stopped.'

She was shaking badly, her knuckles white where her hands were gripping the wheel and she was chewing her bottom lip.

I said, 'Let me drive now, you've done very well.'

When she stopped the car I got out and walked round to the driver's door as she slid across the seat.

She said, 'You've got to tell me what's going on.'

'I will, I promise, but we have to sort out a few more immediate things first.'

There was more than a fair chance that the police had been notified of my crashing act in Waihi. Plenty of people must have seen me run to the Zephyr, realising that it wasn't an accident they'd seen but a deliberate piece of driving. I knew we may have to abandon the car if I wanted to avoid answering questions — questions which I didn't want to answer.

The Zephyr handled very badly. At each turn the back end held back, feeling rather as though we were towing a trailer.

'Does it always corner like this?' I asked.

Karen shook her head. 'No, I thought it felt funny too.'

I thought we might have lost air in the rear tyres during Karen's wheelspin back in Waihi. If the car had tubeless tyres it could easily have happened.

Watching the road, Karen sat tight lipped as I cornered the car as fast as I dared, imagining the tyre getting flatter and flatter with each howl of the rubber.

I had already decided that it would be unwise to drive to Paeroa. The news was bound to have been telephoned ahead and although the township was only tiny, it was more than big enough to be able to provide sufficient police to stop us.

'Get out the map and find me a road into the hills that isn't a dead end,' I said.

Before she had time to move I made up

my mind, braked heavily and turned sharply to the right onto an unsealed road signposted 'Golden Cross'. Maybe it was an omen.

A few minutes later Karen gave me a tight smile 'Good choice,' she said, 'this comes out the other side of Paeroa on the Thames road.'

I shook my head. 'Not so good really — too obvious.'

A small track to the left appeared ahead. Swinging the Zephyr on the loose surface, I drove into a narrow cleft formed by an eroded clay cliff on one side and a tangle of gorse on the other.

'Pause,' I announced, switching off the engine.

I had remembered the first rule of survival — think.

I got out of the car, smelling oil fumes from the hot motor. The off-side rear tyre was very soft.

'Karen,' I shouted, 'come on, we have to change this straight away.'

She walked towards me then stopped, putting her hands on my shoulders to look me in the eyes.

118

'Tell me now,' she said.

I thought I was going to have trouble with Mrs. Hallett.

I said, 'I swear I'll tell you everything but right now we have to get this tyre changed so that we're mobile in case the police find us.'

'Why the police, I thought it was Conway and Monroe you were running from?'

Patiently I said, 'I am not, and was not, running from anyone. Believe it or not I was rescuing you, so please consider yourself saved. The Americans have a very bent motor car that can't follow us but the police have more cars than I can ever smash, and I'm sure they've been fully informed of my deliberate crash back in Waihi, so you and I have to keep out of their way for a bit — okay?'

'I don't feel rescued.'

'I've told you I'll explain — now help me fix the wheel.'

I opened the boot, letting the springs push the lid up.

Karen started to tell me the spare was under the bonnet but stopped at the sight of a large black metal trunk filling most of the compartment.

'What's that?' I asked.

She leant forward, flicked back the two brass catches and lifted the lid.

I pushed her out of the way and ripped open the mouth of one of the canvas sacks that lay inside.

And there it was.

One hundred and fifty thousand dollars worth of gold.

Karen said, 'Oh God.'

I said absolutely nothing, thinking foolishly that it was a beautiful colour.

My nervous fingers fumbled with a cigarette.

I said, 'I've found it for you.'

'Did you know it was in here?'

'No.'

'But Boyd knew?'

I nodded at her.

'He knew all the time — I mean he had — he . . .'

She didn't finish; there was no need.

Then the sobs came, slowly at first and then leaning against the car, she began to cry her heart out.

I let some of the dust run through my fingers. It left a trace of yellow powder in the corner of my nails.

Slamming the trunk shut I closed the boot lid over it. Soft tyre or not I had to get the car hidden now or there was going to be more trouble than I had ever dreamed of. As well as the police, now I had the gold, Boyd, Conway and Monroe would be after us.

Suddenly I wished very much that I had my new Marlin rifle with me.

Gently pulling the girl away from the car I turned her round and lifted her chin. She had stopped crying.

'He lied to me, and to you,' she said bitterly.

'Gold is like that they say.'

'I don't love him, Russ.'

'You did once.'

'You said you'd explain.'

'Some of it's already explained now but you'd better hear the rest. First we have to get the car somewhere where nobody's going to find it though.'

I took her hand and began to walk further along the track. It became progressively more overgrown but still passable for a car if you didn't care about the scratches to the paint work.

I said, 'Go back and bring the car — slowly.'

Further on, the track opened out into what was obviously a disused quarry. Like some kind of primeval monster, the most derelict excavator I have ever seen lay rusting in the bottom.

Apart from the faint sound of running water ahead, the whole area was absolutely still and felt somehow rather evil. I was sure that the quarry was as remote a spot as we could expect to find — especially without looking. Our luck had held again.

Scraping noises heralded the approach of the car.

I waved Karen on, stopping her before the vegetation thinned at the quarry entrance.

Her face was still wet from the tears.

She said, 'Now what?'

'Now I'm going to tell you a true story, come and sit down.'

Sparing no detail I described my

abortive visit to the Bay of Islands including what the Americans had told me about Boyd and gently telling her about her brother.

While I spoke she stared at the ground showing no trace of emotion. There were no more tears, no movement of her body when she heard how David had died.

Her husband had lied to her and the two Americans had murdered her brother. Plans had been made to kidnap her and now the police were probably involved. Right now she was in the middle of nowhere with a carload of illegal gold — it was a hell of a story.

When at last I finished there was still no movement.

Then she looked up quickly her eyes bright and glittering.

'It's funny,' she said. 'I feel nothing about Boyd, I'm not even surprised now I know.'

'I thought you looked pretty happy together.'

'When you've been married a while you can look happy to a visitor in the middle of a flaming row.'

'Oh.'

'You don't care do you?' she said hotly.

'What the hell am I suppose to say to that?'

'I don't know, what are we going to do now?'

I said, 'Think,' and walked back to the car for another cigarette.

Karen came back after I'd smoked half of it. She looked drained and spent.

'I don't want any of the gold ever,' she said.

'You were keen enough a few days ago.'

She shook her head. 'You can have it, Russ.'

I said, 'It's not yours to give. Don't forget Boyd knows you've either stolen it or are driving about in his car not knowing there's a hundred and fifty thousand dollars worth of gold in the boot.'

'So what are you going to do?'

'I don't know.'

There were only two alternatives I could think of. Bury the gold, get rid of the car and take time to decide what to do next, or make a run for it without

124

wasting any more time, soft tyre and all.

I knew if we were picked up it was certain the police would look in the boot and then no amount of ingenious lying would get us out of trouble. Worse still the dust would be gone forever.

In the end I compromised, deciding we would hide the trunk right here and take off in the car for Auckland where at least for a while we could hide in the middle of the city.

The canvas bags containing the dust were at least twice as heavy as anything else of the same size that I had ever carried. There were four of them altogether.

I used a hub cap and a tyre lever to dig a hole in the dry clay under the belly of the old excavator. Not a very good place to conceal the gold, but one which would be easy to find if I came back later in a hurry.

Karen used two more hub caps to carry away the crumbling yellow earth and scattered it in a thin layer over the bed of the quarry pit.

'Can you change the tyre while I finish

this?' I shouted to her.

My fingers were bleeding where the tips had been scraped by digging with the pressed steel dish and my back was screaming enough with each scoop I made.

Ten minutes of digging convinced me it would take too long to excavate a hole large enough to hold the trunk. The canvas bags were going to have to go in as they were.

Eventually I rolled the last one into the shallow pit, treading it into shape before kicking the lumps of clay over the top until the ground was level.

From the car no sign of my work was visible.

Karen had already started replacing the hub caps now that the spare was fitted. There was more colour in her cheeks.

I slammed the bonnet lid, said, 'Get in,' and ran to the driver's door.

Reversing back to the road was more difficult than I expected. Visibility was very poor owing to the gorse that grew from the side of the track spreading its sharp branches right across to the bank.

Once back on the road the sense of urgency reduced somewhat — now all I had to do was avoid any contact with the law.

We proceeded to Golden Cross along the rough metalled road before duly meeting up with the main road to Thames just south of a small township called Hikutaia.

Karen said she thought she could navigate well enough to keep us off the main road once we'd crossed the Waihou river estuary. We had a full tank of gas and with a hundred dollars in my pocket, if we couldn't make Auckland without trouble I wasn't trying.

'Have you any ideas where to stay in Auckland?' I asked.

She paused before answering. 'If we go back to Howick do you think Monroe and Conway would try and kidnap me still?'

'I doubt it, but it doesn't seem worth taking a chance on it.'

'What about Boyd?' she asked quietly.

'You can phone the hotel when we get to Auckland.'

'And say what?'

'Maybe it'd be better if I spoke to him.'

After that we spoke only to argue over Karen's choice of route. Finally when I'd seen enough New Zealand dirt road to last me for some while, we agreed to get back on the main highway. In the dark, the chance of a stray cop noticing a blue Zephyr and deciding it was the one from Waihi was so small that we felt quite safe.

In Otahuhu, near Auckland, I left the car in a free basement garage beneath a new department store before we caught a bus into Queen Street.

Karen had noticed a sign outside an old but respectable house advertising bed and tray.

Wearily trudging back from the bus terminal, I glanced at my watch. It was just past ten o'clock.

The boarding-house smelt musty but there was no dust and the place was neat and tidy. I arranged for a double room in the names of Mr. and Mrs. Crittall from Gisborne.

When we were inside Karen turned on me.

'Why didn't you get two rooms?'

'I get lonely and I'm poor.'

'You'll have to sleep on the floor.'

'Wrong, if anyone's going to sleep on the floor it certainly won't be me.'

We argued stupidly about it and agreed that tomorrow we would buy suitcases so we could check into a hotel — a cheap hotel.

When I phoned Boyd in Waihi, he was not at his hotel.

Later in our room we agreed it had been one hell of a day and both fell promptly asleep side by side on the lumpy bed.

10

Apart from a short but particularly vivid nightmare, I slept extremely well.

Karen looked much the same in the morning. I thought that the real impact of Boyd's betrayal had only just taken effect. Throughout breakfast she remained quiet and withdrawn seeming disinterested in my plans for today.

Not that I had formulated any real plans — just a few thoughts about my future. I carefully avoided thinking about Karen's own marital problems — that was none of my business and there was little I could do.

Several days ago I'd considered the real possibility of having ten per cent of a hundred and fifty thousand dollars to spend. Now I had reason to become a little more ambitious. Karen's husband had deliberately laid a false trail for me, and his partners had beaten me up — I thought fifteen thousand little enough compensation. My new figure alternated between twenty and a hundred thousand — even the whole hundred and fifty thousand could be mine if I wanted to be greedy.

All I had to do was figure out a simple way of selling the gold. Unfortunately, Boyd, Monroe and Conway had given me no real clues to their intentions and I already knew my own ideas were hopelessly impractical.

There was no one in Canada that I knew who could help and nobody in Australia I could trust — I didn't know anyone there well enough anyway.

There was only one person in the whole world who I could rely on absolutely and he lived in the United States — Peter Crittall in San Francisco.

'Karen,' I said, interrupting her silent mood. 'I'm going to take some of it for myself.'

She reached out a hand across the breakfast table to touch my wrist. She said softly, 'You must hate me Russ for what I did to you.'

'I did once, while I still wanted you.'

'What do you feel now?'

'I feel you're fishing for something you'd better leave alone.'

She withdrew.

'Leave the gold alone Russ.'

'No.'

'You never wanted to be rich.'

'I still don't, all I want is enough to pay me well for my trouble and get me settled someplace — a hundred and fifty thousand doesn't make you rich anyway.'

Our conversation dried up. I paid the bill automatically still thinking about Peter Crittall and the gold. We walked out into the Auckland sunshine at nine-thirty both sensing an exaggerated coolness between us.

'I'm going to cable Peter,' I announced.

'What for?'

'To see if he has any contacts in the States that could take the dust — he knows a lot of people on the west coast and I'm sure America is the place to sell.'

'Aren't you worried I might tell Boyd, after all he's still my husband and it's his gold more than yours.'

I didn't answer her. I knew I should

leave the damn stuff where it was if I was smart but I also knew I was no different to the men who had found it in the ground to start with. Karen didn't want anybody to have it, she might try and stop me, but not by involving Boyd. I wondered if she really did still love her husband. Yesterday's outburst could easily have resulted from a sudden taste of sour grapes. One thing I knew for sure; thinking about such things was unlikely to be very profitable.

Inside me I knew there was suppressed attraction and deep longing for Karen Wendle and, as I suspected the same affection existed in part for Mrs. Hallett, they must remain suppressed. I had no intention of going through the same misery all over again. Life is too short and I had enough trouble on my hands already.

'Come on,' I said. 'Enjoy today with me — pretend we're old friends.'

'We are old friends,' she replied without looking at me.

We walked to the Post Office at the bottom of Auckland's Queen Street, becoming less concerned with our problems as we mingled with the noisy crowds.

My cable to Peter read:

'Have inherited all effects from Coromandel Stop Rather dusty but quite valuable Stop If I can ship safely can you sell Stop Write care of Auckland C.P.O. Russ.'

Karen told me I was mad and I agreed with her.

After leaving the clinical splendour of the Post Office building I suggested we walk to the waterfront to discuss what to do next.

'Book in to a hotel as we planned,' I said.

'What for though?'

'Well, I have to live somewhere and until we're sure you've lost your usefulness as a hostage — so do you — I mean you can't go home.'

'I don't want to go home anyway.'

I put five cents into a newspaper box and bought the morning paper. There was nothing about my hit and run accident on the front page of any of the others either.

Seagulls were wheeling above us making their usual raucous screams and I could smell the summer coming clear across the Gulf.

I said, 'I've got to wait to hear from Peter. If he can swing the deal I'll have to figure out some way of smuggling the gold out of the country. It'll take time and you can't stay with me while I'm doing it.'

'Why can't I?'

'Because you're Mrs. Boyd Hallett that's why.'

'I can help you.'

'No, anyway I thought you were against the idea.'

'Don't you want me to stay?'

Wishing desperately I could say yes, but frightened of myself, I gave her a blunt, 'No.'

She winced very slightly and coloured as I deliberately studied her body with my eyes.

'I'll go to my parents' place in Wellington, then,' she said.

I wondered if she knew how I felt about

her still. Now that I had proved to myself that Boyd was a bastard, I seemed to have less of a problem with my emotions. Given half a chance, like a damn fool, I would fall head over heels in love with her again, and I wasn't going to let it happen. Sure she had changed — so had I, but the old feeling was still there.

I said, 'You'd better stay until we either get hold of Boyd or somehow or other make sure you're safe from the Americans.'

'How kind,' she said sarcastically.

After lunch Karen withdrew some cash from her savings account and we bought some used suitcases from a second-hand dealer for an outrageous price, but, as they were considerably cheaper than new ones, it was the only thing to do.

★   ★   ★

I was very worried about my bent rental car, although there was little I could do about it short of admitting to crashing it. Eventually, in view of circumstances, I elected to do nothing.

Karen went off by herself to rent another car — the cheapest she could find, leaving me to find a suitable hotel. We arranged to meet again outside the Chapel of Auckland University in Princes Street.

Surprisingly, accommodation presented a major problem. I didn't fancy one of the large hotels let alone the price, whilst the smaller ones, almost universally, appeared to be scruffy and poorly located.

Exactly at three-thirty Karen arrived in a smart red Mini outside the Chapel to find me exhausted from climbing up and down Auckland's hills.

'I hope you got two rooms,' she said.

'I thought you'd changed your mind about that?'

She didn't answer.

I told her I hadn't found anything suitable.

'A motel then,' she said.

'The last motel you recommended was not a success.'

'There's a new one in Papakura, Russ — we'll go there.'

Papakura I remembered, was about

twenty miles due south of Auckland.

I said, 'Why so far?'

'Because I say so.'

A touch of the old Karen had returned. I climbed into the car realising my back was much improved, it was stiff but that was all.

'Right then, let's go,' I said.

The south Auckland motorway is a splendid road, contrasting markedly with other less grand highways in New Zealand. In no time at all the large green exit sign informed us of our approach to Papakura.

Karen drove directly to the motel, a pleasant ranch style building faced in a particularly attractive yellow stone material.

We took two rooms next to each other, registering as Mr. Brackenridge and his secretary Mrs. Brent — two unoriginal names we invented on the spur of the moment just before we signed the book. Then we drove into Papakura town to find somewhere to have dinner.

I bought an evening newspaper leaving Karen to lock the car and attend to the meter.

Half-way down the front page the thick black print screamed at me.

'Auckland geologist killed at Waihi.' With shaking hands I read on, a coldness creeping over me.

'Mr. Boyd Hallett of Howick was found dead in his hotel room by Waihi police this morning. It is understood the matter is being treated as murder.

'Mr. Hallett recently attended the funeral of his brother-in-law, Mr. David Wendle in Coromandel and is believed to have remained on the peninsula since then.

'Police are anxious to interview his wife Mrs. Karen Hallett and a close friend of the family, Mr. Russ Gallagher, recently arrived from Canada.

'Reports of a motor accident involving Mr. Gallagher's car are thought to be connected with the case.

'Eyewitnesses report that a man answering to the description of Mr. Gallagher deliberately crashed a car into a parked vehicle yesterday morning in Waihi before driving off in a blue Ford Zephyr.

'Any persons having information that could assist the police are asked to telephone the Waihi Central Police Department at once.'

Karen had joined me before I finished reading. When I had scanned the report twice I left her holding the paper and lit a cigarette. I hoped she wouldn't behave hysterically.

Before I had time to return the packet to my pocket Karen was shaking me, her face ashen.

'They killed him — they killed Boyd,' she stuttered.

Quickly I propelled her back to the car, took the key from her handbag and dumped her in the passenger seat.

I drove back to the motel, helped Karen to her room. and locked us both in. It was five-thirty.

She lay on the bed face down leaving me to try and decide how serious our problem really was.

I didn't know what to say to her about her husband. Whilst our recent conversation had convinced me there was no real love for Boyd left, the shock must have been considerable nevertheless.

The situation had snowballed at an unbelievable rate until finally I was now wanted for murder. I had my skin to save as well as hers and I couldn't spend time wondering how genuine her grief was.

I knew if anyone wanted to dig a little, I had the best motive in the world, as well as being involved in a series of events at Waihi that were suspicious to say the least. I was in a real mess.

I said, 'Karen — I know we've been talking all day but we've got to figure out what to do.'

There was no movement on the bed.

I turned over the limp body and sat down beside her.

'We're in trouble, Karen.'

'We can tell the police can't we — we've done nothing wrong.'

'Do you think they'd believe us with all that gold involved?'

She didn't answer.

'What name did you give when you rented the car?' I asked her.

'My own — they ask to see your licence.'

That cut down our time a good deal even though there were a lot of red Minis about. We were going to have to move fast and cautiously. I couldn't even collect an answer from Peter Crittall now, in fact we were in trouble if we moved at all as well as being in danger if we stayed too long in one spot. I was very frightened about what might happen to us.

I said, 'Where's your passport?'

'At home.'

'Damn!'

'Why?'

'I thought we might make a run for it, or a fly for it rather.'

She shook her head slowly. 'Not a chance from the airport and we haven't enough money. You can't change traveller's cheques now and I daren't use my bank account.'

'We can't get Peter's answer from the Post Office.' I said.

'I know.'

'I could phone him,' I said suddenly. 'They won't monitor overseas calls will they?'

Karen looked blank. She said, 'Why would they kill Boyd?'

Anger rose in my throat — to hell with Boyd, he was dead and there wasn't time to analyse what might have happened. I felt sorry for Karen — I thought I did anyway, but if we were going to escape I had to concentrate on that and that alone.

I placed the call at once but was told it would have to be booked, and that it would be at least three hours before there was space available on the line. They would call me.

*　*　*

At nine-thirty the phone rang.

I heard Peter saying, 'Russ, is that you?' and interrupted him at once.

'Peter,' I said, 'how are you? I bet you didn't expect a call from your old mate Rusty Brackenridge in New Zealand.'

That shut him up.

He said, 'I certainly didn't — not at this time of night.'

'Peter, I need a little help — or a lot really and I want it in a great hurry.

143

There's a cable on its way to you — ignore it please — just listen because I only want to say it once.'

Speaking slowly, I said, 'Two of us, the original pair, have inherited the stuff you know about. There is a good deal of trouble about it outside the family and we need assistance to move both it and us. There's about three hundred pounds of it. There's virtually no time left and we can't travel at all. Can you help — there's no one else I can ask.'

Peter said, 'Is it real trouble?'

'The worst.'

'Do you have any documents?'

'Only one of us — me.'

'How long have I got to organise something?'

'Days at the most.'

'Where do I contact you?' he asked.

'Cable Brackenridge care of Papakura Central Post Office.'

There was a slight pause.

I said, 'We could leave the stuff for later.'

'Or forever?'

'If necessary.'

144

He said, 'Anything else?'

'No, just hurry please.'

Peter coughed over the line. 'In that case goodnight to you. I'll start right away. So long, Rusty.'

I said, 'Good night,' and put down the phone.

Karen was sitting on the bed swinging her pretty legs.

She said, 'What can he do?'

'Wait and see.'

So we waited.

11

It was fortunate that our wait did not exceed three days. Being with Karen for virtually all of the time had begun to do strange things to me. I was continually fighting with myself, trying not to give in and reach out for her.

She accepted what comfort I could provide about Boyd, but it was still impossible for me to decide whether she cared or not about his death. Apart from an overwhelming crawling worry about our predicament, my concern was what to do with Karen — if and when our situation were ever to return to normal.

Vague ideas of marriage filtered through my thoughts about gold and of about Boyd's murder. After a couple of days, Karen brightened up a little adopting an attitude of child-like reliance on me, so much so recently that I had become annoyed.

We avoided using the Mini as much as possible, each day driving early in the morning seventeen miles to an east coast beach called Kawakawa Bay, and returning to the motel at dusk.

Then, on the fourth day, when I walked into town from the motel in the morning, there was a cable for me at the Post Office. I took it back to the motel before opening it.

The message was very brief.

'Hiram C. Bernhardt will meet you Papakura C.P.O. 4.30 p.m. October 24th. Peter.'

I read it to Karen.

'Who?' she said.

I passed her the cable.

'Do you know him?' she asked me.

'No, never heard of him — I'd remember someone with a name like that too.'

'It's the twenty-fourth today,' Karen said.

'So we only have to wait until this afternoon.'

She sighed. 'I'm glad. I'm tired of this.'

I thought she couldn't be more tired of waiting than I was, but I didn't say so.

Mr. Bernhardt would be a friend of

Peter's I supposed. I wondered what his proposals were going to be. If he was going to help us out of our current position and recommend a way of selling the gold he would have to be pretty damn smart. I'd spent three days thinking about it and had come up with nothing.

The only way to describe our final day of waiting is to say we wasted it away in frustration until at last it was time for my appointment at the Post Office.

Arriving early, I could see no sign of anyone who could possibly be called Hiram C. Bernhardt, although of course I reluctantly admitted to myself that he might easily be a very ordinary looking guy.

Minutes later a white Ford Falcon drew up to the kerb beside me. A small man with glasses and a bald head peered at me from the open window.

'Mr. Brackenridge?' he enquired politely.

'Yes — are you Mr. Bernhardt?'

'I am — may I give you a lift?'

I walked round to the other door and climbed in.

'How did you recognise me?' I asked.

'Since leaving the plane at Auckland, you are the only person I have seen who looks as though the whole world is at his heels.'

I said, 'Oh,' feeling my confidence slip away.

Bernhardt was very small, rather thin and very unimpressive.

He said, 'Where am I to go please?'

'To the motel where we're staying — turn left just here.'

'We will discuss everything when we arrive,' he said.

'Are you a friend of Peter Crittall?' I asked.

'No.'

'But he asked you to come here?'

'No.'

'I thought you were here to help us.'

'I am here to work, Mr. Brackenridge.'

'My real name's Russ Gallagher.'

'How nice.'

I shut up after that, speaking only to direct him to the motel.

As expected, Karen looked surprised when I introduced Bernhardt to her.

He did not return her smile.

I said, 'I'm afraid I can't offer you a drink or anything.'

'I understand — I should like to hear the whole story at once please.'

He sat down expectantly, squinting short-sightedly at us through his thick glasses.

I felt strongly disinclined to tell this odd character about our recent troubles, on the other hand, I had implicit faith in Peter Crittall and I knew Bernhardt wouldn't be here unless Peter was sure he was the right guy for the job.

'Okay,' I said, 'here goes.'

Sparing no detail, I explained the whole series of events leading up to the point where we had buried the gold and had become wanted by the police in connection with the death of Karen's husband.

When I had finished and Karen had added a couple of small details, Bernhardt rubbed his hands together as though washing them.

'So you wish to leave this rather delightful country without fear of extradition and realise cash on the gold you have acquired?'

Karen and I said, 'Yes' at the same time.

The little man washed his hands again.

'I will explain my proposition to you,' he said.

'Are you a friend of Peter's?' Karen asked.

I said, 'No he's not — let him explain.'

There was the suspicion of a smile at the corner of his mouth. He said, 'I represent a large importing concern in Los Angeles. My organisation deals particularly in diamonds and other precious stones, also in rare metals and occasionally people.'

'What people?' Karen asked.

'Principally Mexicans wishing to live in the United States, but also Germans anxious to cross the Berlin Wall. However, we usually consider contracts requiring the importation or transfer of aliens only if a substantial quantity of stones is involved.'

'Or gold?' I said.

'We have twice dealt in gold from South Africa and once from Australia — our negotiations with both those countries are almost universally concerned with precious stones.'

I said, 'Your dealings, as you call them, are all illegal?'

'I did not say that.'

'What's the company called?' I asked.

'Diamond Importers — why do you ask?'

I was confused. How on earth had Peter come across such people? Karen was looking as worried as I felt.

The little man sensed our obvious concern.

He said, 'I can assure you that I can make all the necessary arrangements for you. Whilst the quantity of gold involved in this instance is extremely small and we would not usually be interested, on this occasion I have been instructed by our manager to offer every assistance. I have the contract here for you to sign.'

From his light-weight travel case he produced a large folded document which he passed to me.

It began — 'The tape recording that has just been taken is quite safe with our representative. It has been recorded as a precaution only and is intended to safeguard the interests of Diamond Importers. It will be given to you or to a representative of your Company or Organisation either at the satisfactory completion of this contract or immediately if you do not wish to proceed.'

There was a perforated line across the vellum sheet followed by an ordinary official contract form containing a general agreement clause which was to be signed by both parties.

I read the document twice.

'You must be joking,' I said.

'Am I to understand you do not wish to sign any such agreement, Mr. Brackenridge?' he asked.

'Gallagher.'

'As you please.'

'It's just a little unexpected I'm afraid,' I muttered awkwardly, wondering what was coming next. 'I'm not very used to things like this.'

Bernhardt appeared displeased.

He said, 'I have already explained that you are fortunate to be offered a contract for such a small quantity of metal.'

'How much then?' I said.

'For guaranteed safe passage of you and Mrs. Hallett to the United States and transportation of the gold to Los Angeles as the property of Diamond Importers — sixty per cent of the current United States market price for the metal.'

'Sixty per cent!'

'That is correct.'

'All right,' Karen spoke suddenly, 'don't be silly, Russ, Peter knows what he's doing, he wouldn't have contacted these people if he thought there was a better way.'

'But that's over half.'

'You're forgetting none of it's yours really.'

Three days ago I would have laughed at the idea of losing sixty per cent of the gold just to sell it but, I was tired of the worry and frightened that Karen and I would be arrested for Boyd's murder. This way at least we'd get out of New Zealand and have a little cash left. I fancied that Diamond Importers knew their business rather well.

I said, 'You can get it out of New Zealand?'

'Yes, with your help.'

'What about us?'

'I anticipate little problem.'

'If I sign the contract, how do I know you won't copy the tape?'

'You do not, but I would point out that Diamond Importers have no wish to be involved with any unethical negotiations for very obvious reasons. It is possible that you may feel resentful at what you consider to be an excessive percentage once you have reached the United States safely and subsequently attempt to cause trouble. This contract is intended to prevent such an unfortunate occurrence.'

It was very smooth and very organised. The odd external appearance of Mr. Hiram C. Bernhardt obviously concealed a shrewd and experienced operator, well versed in international smuggling on a huge scale. I thought Diamond Importers would be a very prosperous company.

'Oh hell,' I said, 'I guess it's a deal.'

I stuck out my hand to Bernhardt who

placed a ball point pen in it and pointed to his damn contract.

Karen signed immediately beneath me.

We sat down again, waiting for our instructions while he scribbled his own name.

Bernhardt had taken a few short notes earlier in the meeting. He now began to read from them.

'Tonight,' he said, 'your rental car will be returned to Auckland, we will use mine from now on. You will leave the motel as soon as possible and the three of us will move at once into more suitable accommodation. It will be necessary for you to guide me in that respect.

'After I have purchased the materials that will be required, we will collect the gold and both of you will undertake the processing leaving me to negotiate your passage to the United States. I do not believe that things will take long to arrange.

'There are a few minor questions I must ask you first.'

'What?' I said rather sharply.

'Firstly, have I your word that neither

you nor Mrs. Hallett were in any way directly involved in the death of Mr. Hallett?'

I said, 'You have.'

'My company attempts to avoid unnecessary contact with civil authorities and does not condone either violence or drug trafficking.'

'Good of them,' I said.

He went on, 'Secondly, what is the relationship between you?'

Karen answered quickly, 'We are very old friends — I was going to marry Russ once.'

'And now?' enquired Mr. Bernhardt.

'Now,' I spat at him, 'we are suspected of murder and wish to get the hell out of here with a little cash so that we can think of such things.'

The half-smile was at his mouth again.

'I see,' he said.

Karen looked at me sideways.

He said, 'There will be an expensive house to rent in this evening's papers, I imagine?'

'I guess so,' I answered.

'It is essential that it has a bath.'

'Would you like a shower here?' Karen asked.

'You do not understand.'

'No we don't,' I said.

Mr. Bernhardt said he would drive into Papakura to collect some food and an evening newspaper. We watched him go with feelings of relief.

'I don't believe he exists,' Karen announced.

'He does,' I said.

'All of a sudden we're part of an organised international smuggling thing, being ordered about by a little man who knows all the tricks of the trade,' Karen said unhappily.

I said, 'You were right all along — I should've left it alone. Boyd would still be alive and we wouldn't be mixed up with Diamond Importers if I'd listened to you.'

'Is it too late, Russ?'

'Yeah, I think it is now — we're going to have to go the whole way just to stop going to court for Boyd.'

'I'm sure if we told the truth it would be all right.'

I shook my head. 'I'd like to believe you but I've told you before, without having Conway and Monroe under lock and key I wouldn't want to take a chance on it.'

An hour later Bernhardt returned carrying three large cardboard pots of Chinese food and the paper.

'I have marked several properties that are for rent,' he said, 'I would like Mrs. Hallett to decide which of them would be the most suitable. The principle requirement is exclusiveness.'

When we had finished eating, Bernhardt and I left the motel to drive to Auckland to dump the rented Mini leaving Karen to telephone four houses advertised for rent. She had instructions to arrange viewing as early in the morning as possible.

Later that night, when we returned to the motel, Karen told us she had provisionally rented a five bedroomed house in St. Heliers, an expensive area on the waterfront in south Auckland city. By telephone she had arranged for Bernhardt to call at the agents in the morning with two months rent in advance plus a bond of a hundred dollars.

Bernhard said she had done well and that if possible we would move in tomorrow so that we could begin working at once.

He retired early to the spare bed in my room with a cup of coffee and the phone book to read.

12

The house at St. Heliers was as splendid as we expected for a rental of forty-eight dollars a week.

Bernhard stayed long enough to carry out a brief investigation of the premises before roaring off in the car saying that he hoped to return by lunch time.

As good as his word, at midday the Falcon reappeared with the back seat covered in groceries and the boot lid tied down over something large and oily.

Tall bushes screened the driveway of our new house, allowing Karen and I to help with the unloading without fear of being recognised by inquisitive neighbours.

Unexpectedly, the boot contained an antiquated and extremely rusty pair of metal rollers — the kind used for forming sheet metal into curves. Karen thought it was a giant mangle from an old washing machine.

Also in the car, still in their cartons, were four brand new electric fan heaters, arousing my curiosity still further.

After a quick lunch which Karen prepared from the food Bernhardt had brought, he was off again with a promise to be back before dark.

'He's not so bad really,' Karen remarked soon after he'd left.

'I suppose at least he's working for his money,' I said, wondering what extraordinary paraphernalia he would bring back this evening.

I could never have guessed. At five o'clock, we welcomed Bernhardt home again with a hundred pounds of sugar and an enormous roll of industrial brown paper filling the gaping boot.

The paper roll must have weighed in excess of five or six hundred pounds alone. It was nearly three feet in diameter and about four feet wide.

On the back seat lay three more cardboard boxes.

'Would you be kind enough to put those in the garage, Mr. Brackenridge,' he said.

Two of the boxes held shiny new car jacks wrapped in oily paper whilst the third contained a small but well built hoist combining a particularly compact pulley system with a length of heavy nylon rope. I thought it would be designed for lifting out car engines — especially useful for the enthusiastic amateur.

Karen called us in for dinner before I had time to ask him to explain the use of his strange purchases.

When we were seated he smiled happily at us both — it was the first time. We smiled back.

'I will explain,' he said.

'In order to ship the gold dust out of New Zealand and into the United States it is of course essential to disguise or conceal it in some way. If it is to be hidden, experience has shown that a fundamental requirement is the use of a carrier commodity well known as an export item from the country concerned. Further, the selected commodity should be relatively inexpensive and innocuous in appearance. New Zealand is particularly well known for dairy products, wool and timber. My principals in Los Angeles have considered the possibility of hollow pine in some detail, although the idea might at first sight appear ludicrous or impractical.

'There is difficulty in easily providing concealed volume in a number of logs but the idea has some merit. However, New Zealand is also well known for its pulp and paper industry and it is with this that we are concerned on this occasion.'

'Brown paper,' I said.

'Yes — the roll in the car. The principal use for such paper both here and in the United States is in the manufacture of decorative and industrial laminate — Formica is an excellent example. Sheets of paper are coated and impregnated with resin before being heated under pressure to form a hard rigid surface.

'A roll of raw paper is heavy, cheap and a high volume export item, it will not attract attention anywhere in the world. Because of its weight, the addition of three hundred pounds of gold is unlikely to be noticed by the drivers of fork lift trucks or the controllers of other mechanised handling equipment. You will also agree that it is an unlikely medium for the illegal transportation of gold.'

I said, 'Most unlikely.'

Bernhardt nodded and continued. 'Providing a hollow section in the roll is difficult and by no means foolproof. It is better to distribute the gold uniformly over the entire surface of the paper and to re-roll it. In that way, the chances of detection by X-rays are much reduced and the subsequent recovery of the metal is not really complicated to any extent.

'You, Mr. Brackenridge, with Mrs. Hallett's help, are going to impregnate and coat the roll of paper I have bought with a solution of sugar and water mixed with gold dust. The film will be dried by domestic fan heaters, and the paper re-rolled before forwarding it by sea to one of the major manufacturers of decorative laminate in the United States. Once there, Diamond Importers will collect the roll and reclaim the dust by dissolving the sugar adhesive. The system is extremely inexpensive, readily carried out by two or three people with a minimum of equipment, and most reliable.'

'Where did you get the paper?' Karen asked.

'From the local Formica factory — the manager was most helpful.' Bernhardt smiled his half-smile. 'Polyvinyl alcohol would have been much better than sugar for a water soluble adhesive but I was unable to buy any locally I'm afraid.'

I told the little man I was impressed.

He said. 'It will call for some hard work to coat the paper I fear. I suggest you mix the solution in the bath after jamming the rolling machine against the sides so that the rollers are as far as possible below the surface of the liquid.

'The paper must pass slowly over the heaters to thoroughly dry it before re-rolling.

'It may be necessary to process the roll more than once — remembering that the first twenty feet should be left uncoated in case there is control inspection at the port of entry.'

Having been presented with a system like this I couldn't wait to begin. I said,

'We'll set it up tonight and get the gold tomorrow — is that okay?'

Mr. Bernhardt thought that would be an excellent programme and proceeded to remove his jacket in preparation for the evening's work.

It was dusk by the time we had manoeuvred the roll out of the car boot onto the ground.

The little hoist was not really adequate for the job and at one time I had a dreadful feeling that the wooden beam in the garage would give way under the load. But after an anxious half-hour, our roll was ready to be pushed and manhandled round to the sliding doors of the lounge. One carefully timed heave by the three of us and it lay comfortably on the carpet, looking very incongruous in such elegant surroundings.

Bernhardt produced two five-foot lengths of large diameter steel water pipe, some pieces of wood, a hammer and a box of nails.

'I picked up these this morning,' he explained. 'I forgot they were in the car.'

We used the car jacks and bricks to lift the roll from the floor after passing one of the steel pipes through the hollow centre of the cardboard former.

Bernhardt slid two very nice chairs under the ends of the pipe and, with utter disregard for the furniture, drove in a cluster of nails each side of the spindle to keep it in place.

Leaving Karen to carefully peel off the outer wrapping which she was instructed to preserve for re-use, Bernhardt and I planned the route of the paper to the bathroom and back again.

He supported the second length of water pipe on another chair, the free end being jammed into a hole hammered in the plaster board covering of the lounge wall.

It was going to be necessary to twist the paper as it passed through doorways but I could see no major problem in this, providing the re-rolling was done slowly and carefully.

Leaning on the second water pipe he paused for a moment to think.

He said, 'We will reel the dry paper onto this spindle first and then hope that one pass through the solution will pick up all the gold at one attempt before winding it back onto the original cardboard former.'

'Have you got any idea how much sugar-water mixture we need?' I asked.

'I have been advised that a roll of this length will use about forty-five gallons of liquid,' he answered briefly.

Karen had to help us carry the rolling machine to the bathroom and wedge it in place in the bath. It was impossible to avoid chipping the enamel. The house was beginning to look something of a mess when we'd finished our preparations.

Finally, we were ready to transfer the dry paper onto what was to be our take-off spool.

With both hands, Karen began to turn the roll, spilling paper onto the floor so that Bernhardt and I could re-roll it onto our water pipe across the other side of the room.

It was unnecessary to do this neatly and a few strategically placed arm chairs and coffee tables allowed the whole job to be completed in less than a couple of hours.

A pause for coffee and biscuits was most welcome. I felt better than I'd felt for several days, the action was revitalising me and creating the old sense of adventure.

'Hadn't we better try it through the rollers going the proper way?' Karen asked.

I said. 'I'm worried about it creasing when it's wet before we get to the bank of heaters, but as we can't wet it before we're ready for the real run, I suppose there's nothing we can do.'

We tried it dry. By midnight, with me winding the handle of the rolling machine and Karen reeling onto the cardboard former by hand, the web of paper was moving like a charm.

Lengths of cord were used to support the paper as it passed over the heaters as we believed the additional weight of solution might cause it to sag. Bernhardt was worried about the possibility of gold being scraped off, but I thought the film would probably tend to stay on the paper rather than build up on the cord to an undesirable thickness.

Eventually all of us staggered off to bed, believing we had done an honest day's work although, in actual fact, nothing could have been further from the truth.

For the first time since I'd been in New Zealand, with genuine affection, Karen kissed me goodnight.

★　★　★

New Zealand produced one of its sour days the following morning. Last night, plans had been made for Bernhardt and I to collect the gold from the quarry today, leaving Karen to experiment with an electric food mixer as a stirrer for our one hundred and fifty thousand dollar mixture.

Details of how Karen and I were to be transported to California had not been discussed and, on the early morning drive to Golden Cross, the man from Diamond Importers seemed unwilling to talk about it.

He drove fast in the heavy rain, but not dangerously — being careful to observe the speed limits in towns and villages. We talked a good deal and there were many questions about Monroe and Conway which I was unable to answer, having only a brief association with the two gentlemen.

The rain abated a little before we turned onto the loose metal, but we were still going to get very wet when the time came to recover the buried sacks of gold.

I directed him to the entrance of the clay road and then left the protection of the car to walk ahead, pushing my way through the wet gorse to check the surface.

Through the rain the excavator still looked like a monster, but it made finding the hiding place very easy.

Soaked to the skin and covered in sticky yellow clay we slipped and slithered with the heavy canvas bags, dumping them unceremoniously into the boot of the waiting Falcon.

We spoke little on the drive back to St. Heliers. I was busy with my own thoughts and I guess Hiram C. Bernhardt was busy with his.

I wondered how much of the sixty per cent he would get — perhaps that was what he was thinking about.

At four o'clock we turned into the white concrete driveway leading to the house, waving to Karen waiting at the back door.

'Have you got it?' she asked.

Bernhardt looked surprised.

He said, 'Of course Mrs. Hallett.'

I grinned at her. 'Is the processing plant ready?'

'Of course, Mr. Gallagher.'

She had already filled the bath with hot water in which all the sugar had been dissolved. The mixer lay ready on the floor.

'I hammered the plug in,' she said, 'wouldn't it be terrible if it came out and the gold went down the drain.'

'Did the mixer work okay?' I asked.

'It helped dissolve the sugar but I don't know if it'll stop the dust from settling on the bottom.'

Bernhardt said, 'Although gold is an extremely dense metal, when in particle form it will be easier to keep it in

173

suspension than you think — at least, that is what I have been led to believe.'

Karen cooked steak for dinner. Even Bernhardt seemed anxious to get on with the job and we didn't linger at the table, all agreeing that the sooner we started the better.

I was reluctant to tip the yellow dust into the water. I didn't know what else to do with it, but it seemed quite wrong to pour all that money into a common bath tub — especially when there was a rusty set of old sheet metal rollers sitting in the water already.

Obviously, Bernhardt did not suffer from any such foolish reservations. He sat the bottom of one bag on the edge of the bath, tipping the contents into the water in one long continuous golden stream.

Ashamed of my hesitation I poured my bag in, following it quickly with the two others.

The three of us swirled the water about with our hands until even the finest particles of dust were wetted and ready to sink when the water became calm.

To the amusement of Bernhardt, when

174

we had finished, Karen rinsed her gold plated hands under the tap.

'We will waste a great deal Mrs. Hallett — I should not worry if you have fifty dollars worth under your nails.'

The fan heaters had not been tried before. Two of them were positioned immediately beneath the path of the paper whilst the other pair had been suspended from a length of timber so that a blast of hot air was directed downwards in order to dry the top surface of the paper as it passed by.

Four fan heaters provide about eight kilowatts of heat; I thought we were going to be rather warm whilst we worked.

Karen was put in charge of re-reeling, I manned the rollers in the bath while Bernhardt was responsible for creating maximum turbulence in the fluid, using the food mixer with extension beaters made of fencing wire crudely tied onto the existing shafts.

'Are we right?' I enquired.

There were nods.

Slowly I began to turn the handle on the rollers feeling the load as the paper pulled tight from the reel.

Karen picked up the end of the web as it left the bath and began to walk backwards, supporting it on the network of cords after it had been passed over the bank of heaters. Soon she vanished from sight in the direction of her reeling station.

'You're going too fast,' she shouted from the lounge. 'It's not dry enough.'

Turning the rollers slowly proved more difficult than turning them quickly. I had to keep an even tension on the paper to prevent the generation of slack between the roll and the bath. It was a trick that was quickly learned.

After several feet had been wound through, Bernhardt decided the support cords were not necessary. Our fan heaters could be arranged at angles, so that the paper rode nicely on a cushion of low pressure hot air — a well known method of transporting light films.

There was no doubt that the system worked. The material looked exactly like brown paper recently sprayed with gold paint.

176

'I bet we're the only people in the world doing this tonight,' I grinned at Bernhardt.

He replied with the half smile. 'Not only that, Mr. Brackenridge, but a mental calculation I have just made leads me to suggest that we may be the only people doing this tomorrow night as well.'

'Are we going to process the whole roll in one go?' I asked.

He nodded. 'I think it would be advisable. We cannot let the paper be submerged for very long or it will become too sodden and weak, and it would be better not to have to lift the rollers from the bath.'

So we carried on. Bernhardt had the worst job trying to prevent the gold from settling whilst attempting to create an even gold-sugar-water mixture adjacent to the rollers. The rollers themselves worked quite well although they were worn badly in the middle, leaving a thicker layer of wet dust and adhesive along the centre of the paper. At the edges, where the steel cylinders nipped the paper, particles of gold were forced into the surface by the pressure. Occasionally, an odd lump of the soft material would be picked up from the solution and flattened as it passed through the rolls. Karen said she rolled one up worth a dollar.

With aching muscles we continued, the whir of the mixer, the clank of the rollers and the hum from the heaters filling our heads, whilst our unseeing eyes focused on the never ending web of gold-spangled paper moving slowly across the room.

13

I don't think we would have been able to repeat the process a second time. At midnight, even Bernhardt admitted to a desire to pull out the bath plug and dump the remaining solution down the drain. But he didn't, and we carried on until it was obvious that we had more paper than we needed to absorb the mixture.

At five o'clock in the morning, the bath ran dry with about a hundred feet of paper remaining on the water pipe. With immense relief we lifted the rollers from the empty bath, deciding unanimously to finish reeling the unused paper when we had rested.

Physically and mentally exhausted, we collapsed gratefully onto our beds and tried to sleep.

Hours later Karen woke me up with a cup of coffee a pile of hot toast and marmalade.

'What time is it?' I asked.

She looked at her watch. 'Just gone three o'clock.'

I groaned, burying my head in the pillow.

She said, 'Bernhardt's already gone out.'

'He didn't have to wind that miserable handle all night.'

'Drink your coffee Russ — you'll feel better.'

In fact, I felt more awake afterwards, but not better.

I walked into the lounge to find Karen. She was winding the remaining paper methodically onto the reel.

'How can you?' I winced.

'Come on — help me, there's only a bit left to do.'

When we had finished, we wrapped up the most expensive roll of paper in the world using the original protective covering, before lowering the finished article onto the floor by means of the car jacks.

'It's finished,' I said, 'all we have to do now is decide how to spend our forty per cent.'

Karen was not so optimistic. She said

reservedly, 'Don't count our chickens Russ — we're not safe yet, not so long as the police still want to see us about Boyd. You're the one who keeps on telling me that.'

I said, 'I have great faith in Hiram C. Bernhardt. Anyone who works for an outfit that thought of smuggling gold like this should be able to whisk us to L.A. on a magic carpet.'

'I'm not sure if I want to go.'

'What?'

'To America.'

I groaned. 'You've got no choice Karen, why for God's sake start wondering now?'

'What are we going to do in L.A.?'

I'd been dreading the question, knowing it would come sooner or later and knowing I didn't have an answer yet. Or did I?

I knew she was serious this time. She was waiting for me to speak.

And then suddenly I knew that there was no point in fooling myself any longer. To hell with waiting. If things went wrong, which they still could, I would never forgive myself.

Many times in my life I've wished I'd lived for one particular day instead of always planning ahead. Now, in the most unusual personal circumstances I could ever expect to experience, I decided to hell with tomorrow.

I crossed the room to the girl I used to love.

She was looking at me in a strange way — almost as if she was frightened.

'How long's Boyd been dead?' I asked her. 'As a husband, I mean.'

She dropped her eyes to the ground.

I gathered the long black hair and held it gently behind her neck; then, placing my other hand beneath her chin, I lifted her head making her look at me.

For a moment she refused to meet my eyes. When I was ready to back off and crawl away she suddenly moved back from me to stand solemnly, hands by her side with her breasts heaving beneath the thin cotton dress.

She was staring at me, eyes bright and glittering as only hers can do. 'For nearly three years,' she said slowly. 'I tried to tell you.'

Taking hold of myself, I said, 'I promised myself I wasn't going to do this again, I'm not the sort of guy to put my hand in the fire twice — even if I do want something very much.'

She said, 'You're talking in riddles.'

'Because I'm scared.'

'I'm frightened too.'

I said, 'You say it.'

She moved close to me, put her arms gently round my neck and whispered, 'I love you so much I can't live without you ever again.'

Years of suppressed emotion flowed through my body, melting my senses as I held Karen tightly to me, wondering that I could still feel like this after fighting it for so long.

She was crying softly, repeating my name over and over again while we clutched each other. In a little while she stopped crying, using my handkerchief to dry her eyes. We didn't let go of each other.

Now that it was done, I felt as though an immense burden had been lifted from me. I whirled her round the room holding her by the waist, laughing when we became tangled in the pieces of gold coated cord lying on the carpet.

Bernhardt found us behaving like a couple of children. He said, 'You are celebrating the completion of the roll?'

'We are,' I replied, 'we are celebrating very hard.'

He produced an envelope from his case.

'Could you suspend festivities until you have signed these and had your photographs taken please?'

'What are they?' Karen asked, holding up two pieces of thick blue paper.

'Inserts for British passports, Mrs. Hallett. There is one for you and one for Mr. Brackenridge.'

'British passports?' I queried.

'They are easier to buy than New Zealand passports — there are also many more of them for sale.'

'But you can't buy a passport,' Karen looked surprised.

Bernhardt gave her a half-smile. 'Of course you can — anything can be purchased — anything at all. I have yet to encounter that which cannot be bought — it is all a question of money — nothing else.'

I said, 'You're going to buy two British passports for us and substitute our names and photos?'

'That is correct, although it is somewhat more complicated than you have suggested — I will have them ready tomorrow or the day after.'

A few days ago I would have been astonished to hear Bernhardt talk so easily about forged passports, now, it seemed perfectly natural that he would arrange matters so efficiently.

Still holding Karen's hand, I sat down to sign my name on the slip of paper. It was also necessary to fill in particulars of my occupation, my height, colour of hair and the colour of my eyes.

'It would be easier if you sign as husband and wife,' Bernhardt said.

'Mr. Robert Morgan and his wife Elizabeth,' Karen laughed, 'go on, Russ — I've decided I want to be Elizabeth Morgan.'

Bernhardt took our photographs with a

Polaroid camera, brushing aside my comment that Polaroid photos were not permitted in passports.

For our photos, we were both required to pad our cheeks slightly with small shaped pieces of expanded polystyrene. With Karen's hair tied in a tight bun and mine combed untidily forward, to our surprise, the small inflation of our cheeks substantially altered our appearance.

Bernhardt explained that he had already arranged for a truck to collect our roll of paper tomorrow morning. It would be driven to Auckland wharf where, with the aid of some cleverly prepared letters, Bernhardt would explain that it had missed the main delivery from the paper factory. I never doubted his ability to convince the authorities for a moment.

'When does it leave?' I asked him.

'In two day's time — I leave the day after.'

Karen stopped giggling. 'What about us?' she said

'A further day will elapse before you leave New Zealand by a routine flight

186

from Auckland — there will be no trouble I'm sure.'

'I figured it would be safer by sea,' I said.

'Why did you think that Mr. Brackenridge?'

'Gallagher,' I said.

'Morgan,' Karen laughed. She had regained her delight.

I was too happy to argue with Bernhardt. If he thought it would be okay he was probably right, and I didn't know why it would be safer by sea anyway.

I said, 'If we fly to L.A. and the roll of paper goes by sea how are we going to collect our cheque?'

Bernhardt looked upset. He said, 'I shall weigh the roll at the wharf, deduct the weight of paper and sugar leaving a figure which will be the nominal weight of the gold.'

I said, 'Won't it still be a bit damp?'

'If it is, Mr. Brackenridge, my calculation will be in your favour.'

After that I stopped worrying about the arrangements — after all there was nothing I could do, whether I agreed with them or not.

Karen and I held hands whilst we discussed our plans for the future.

The man from Diamond Importers was not lacking in human perception. One of his rare and genuine smiles preceded his congratulations.

'What do you mean?' Karen said.

'I am glad you have stopped fencing with each other — I am pleased you are both so happy.'

So we told him all about it and good old Hiram disappeared for a moment to return from the car with a bottle of champagne.

'I had bought this to celebrate the export of the gold,' he explained, 'however, perhaps it would be more appropriate to use it as a toast to the new Mr. and Mrs. Morgan.'

Karen gave him a kiss and I solemnly shook hands. The whole thing was ludicrous, but we all acted our parts with genuine enjoyment, finishing the bottle just before dinner that evening. Afterwards, Karen and I went for a short walk in the garden, leaving Bernhardt to have a well deserved early night.

We talked of many things — foolish things, plans of our new home in America or Canada and of each other.

At ten-thirty, with the New Zealand spring night cool around us, we walked back towards the french doors of the lounge.

'Do I kiss you goodnight here?' I asked.

'Yes,' she replied shyly. 'But as I only married Mr. Morgan this afternoon it would be nice to be kissed in the bedroom as well.'

I lifted her easily into my arms and carried the girl I had loved for eight long years into the protective warmth of the house.

The next two days passed quickly enough. After struggling with my feelings for so long, the happiness that now was mine was sweet beyond belief. New Zealand blessed us with warm clear sunshine whilst Karen and I moved about the house and garden totally caught up in our own world. I cannot remember ever being so happy.

Our roll of paper was collected as arranged, Bernhardt going off with the driver for the remainder of the morning. Later that afternoon we were presented with two well used British passports, two airline tickets and a thousand dollars in cash for each of us. Bernhardt advised us to keep the documents with us at all times from now on. Karen gave her money to me. She had been concerned about her dog Crystal and asked if Bernhardt could arrange with the kennel for the animal to be found a good home.

There was no problem at the warehouse on the wharf, I hadn't expected one. By now, nothing that Bernhardt did surprised me and I had implicit faith in his ability to organise anything.

On the evening of October the thirtieth, the three of us drove to the air terminal in Bernhardt's comfortable Falcon. We said good-bye there after receiving our instructions on how to contact him in Los Angeles when we arrived.

My earlier fears that the whole deal was suspect no longer bothered me. Although it would be the easiest thing in the world for Bernhardt to vanish with the gold and turn us in to the New Zealand police, I was sure he wouldn't. It was possible that Diamond Importers did not exist and that Bernhardt was a lone operator, but that didn't matter. I was sure Peter Crittall wouldn't have put us in the hands of a doubtful organisation or person as far as reliability was concerned.

I shook hands with him outside the car.

'Thank you for all you've done,' I said, meaning it.

'It has been my pleasure, Mr. Brackenridge — I have enjoyed my brief visit — perhaps I can show you and Mrs. Hallet something of California when you arrive.'

He walked away across the floodlit car park, a tiny, insignificant little man with a small suitcase in one hand and his lightweight travel case in the other.

14

On the way back Karen insisted on stopping at her house in Howick to collect a few things before we left the next day.

In the dark, the house at Marine Parade looked exactly the same as it had done the last time I was here. Being what New Zealanders call a right of way section, it was set back well from the road with the driveway passing between two neighbouring homes, each having road frontage. Quietly I reversed down the drive, threatening Karen that I'd drive away without her if she hadn't reappeared in five minutes as promised.

'No you won't — but I'll only be a minute — really.'

I said, 'Don't put on the lights in the house — use the flashlight,' and then she was gone, a slim figure running across the lawn, barely visible in the darkness.

My watch said it was only nine o'clock

and the neighbouring houses all blazed with light. In some of them I could see the blue flicker of television reflected from walls and ceilings.

From the bottom of the cliff, distant waves were breaking on the beach, by the sound of them only small ones. The tide would be out, leaving a wide flat expanse of sand over which little waves would be rolling, causing the gentle rippling I could hear.

Just before five minutes past nine I went to remind Karen of her promise.

Before I reached the base of the steps the scream echoed from the house. It was a long drawn out scream of terror followed by another and then another.

Adrenaline shot into my blood stream as instinct took over. In one bound I was at the open glass doors of the lounge and inside the house.

The scream had come from the bedroom but there was no one there. Frantically I ran through the building turning on the lights in every room and shouting 'Karen' despairingly.

She was gone.

My heart pumped furiously. I was sick with fright for her.

'Karen,' I yelled, 'Karen.'

Doors were banging in the houses all around. More lights flashed on and people were shouting.

Desperately trying to think, I decided quickly that the only way anyone could have left the property unnoticed was by way of the driveway whilst I was inside the house.

Jumping from the patio to the lawn I ran to the car — but too late.

With gravel spurting from the rear tyres, the dark shape of a familiar Chrysler accelerated backwards towards the parked Falcon.

Abandoning my course, I charged for the moving vehicle, reaching the door handle as the solid rear bumper crashed up over the one on the Falcon, crushing the whole front of Bernhardt's car.

The impact tore the door handle from my grasp, causing me to stumble against the grass verge of the lawn and fall heavily onto my side. By the time I was on my feet again, the Chrysler was disappearing towards the road.

A woman was screaming, 'Phone the police,' and I heard a man's voice shout, 'There's still someone there.'

I had two choices. Risk trying to start the battered Falcon or run.

In a densely populated area like Howick, running wasn't going to get me very far. Wrenching open the door of the car I turned the key to operate the starter.

A terrible grinding noise came from the front of the engine followed by an ominous silence. I tried once more with even less success. It was dead.

Three men were advancing nervously down the drive from the road. If the Falcon had started I would have run them down without a second thought.

Vaulting over a low fence into the adjoining property, I moved swiftly across the back garden out onto the road. Then, as fast as I could, I began running down the slope of Marine Parade knowing that I mustn't be caught between the edge of the cliff and the row of houses. No one followed me.

The sirens weren't long coming. There

was still over a quarter of a mile to go before I reached the first intersection, where there was a chance of hiding in the back streets, when the first wail sounded.

Half a mile away two cars were converging on me.

With a desperate sprint I reached the cover of a narrow strip of grass which skirted the edge of the cliff and threw myself flat a moment before the first car screamed round the curve in the road, flooding everything with dazzling light.

There was time for me to roll further into the grass before the second car swept by.

Dangerously close to the crumbling edge of the cliff, I lay with my face on the earth, sobbing with rage and helplessness. But there wasn't time for self-pity, nor was there time to dwell on what had happened to Karen.

The excited barking of dogs at the Hallets' house told me I had perhaps five minutes before they found me.

Already tired, my heart was beating painfully in my chest, and my lungs were unable to meet the demand I had placed upon them.

Karen had only one chance — me. If I was caught, there would be no way of rescuing her. God knows what Conway and Monroe might do to her unless I could find them. But first I had to save myself.

I hadn't expected the police to bring dogs immediately, they would outrun me in no time. There was only one thing to do, a dangerous, foolish thing to attempt, but it might guarantee my freedom at least for a while.

Drawing on hidden reserves of energy, my breath rasping audibly in my throat, I ran for my life and for Karen's.

The dogs were gaining on me.

Then to my left I saw what I was looking for. A minor slip or subsidence of the cliff edge.

Now only about twenty feet above the beach, the height still looked frightening in the dark.

On my back, with stones ripping my shirt, I slid violently down the steep clay and sandstone slope.

I was half-way to the sea, running through puddles left in the sand before the dogs reached the cliff top. Their excited barking increased in volume and frequency as they picked up my fleeting figure in the dim moonlight.

With the sea tugging at my legs, making it difficult to maintain my headlong rush, I gasped in pain with the effort of breathing until at last I fell forward into the cushion of cool water, and began swimming away from the shore, towards the dark shapes of the islands in the Gulf.

Later, when I turned round to face the land, flashlight beams were stabbing into the dark, but their direction was wrong and I was too far out for them to pick out my figure in the water.

My breathing had eased by now, I had not swum quickly — mainly because I was already exhausted but also because my clothes and shoes were a great hindrance in the water.

When I was half a mile from the beach I turned south, feeling the incoming tide help me travel down the coast past

Howick township. All along the shore, there was a blaze of light and I could see vehicles travelling over the gentle coastal hills. Some of them, I knew, would be police cars.

I doubted if they would bother with a launch. In the dark it would be almost impossible to find a lone swimmer without having some idea of his direction of travel.

Using a slow crawl, trying to rest as much as possible between strokes, I used the buoyancy of the water to cradle my body and recover from my earlier exertion. The slowness with which I moved allowed me to think.

The Americans must have had the house staked out. After so long — I worked it out at eight days — they must have wondered if they were wasting their time waiting for one of us to call. In fact, in their position, knowing the police might be watching too, I was surprised they had taken the risk of hanging about Marine Parade every day and night. On the other hand, there was no other possible way of trying to find us, short of hoping that the law would capture us first, which would be no help at all to Conway and Monroe.

Now they had Karen — ironically succeeding after I'd fouled up their first attempt at Waihi.

I had removed my shoes, tying the laces together so I could hang them round my neck, but I had left my clothes on for insulation. It would have been easy to let the heavy sodden garments pull me gently below the surface — they say drowning is not unpleasant. But I couldn't desert Karen or the sweet memory of her. God knows how I would find her but I was going to try. For three or four hours, floating and swimming alternately, I moved painfully slowly away from the lights of Howick and Cockle Bay. When I knew the cold had penetrated the very core of my bones, summoning my last reserves, I struck out for the shore feeling my numb toes strike mud when I had only covered half the distance to the line of trees ahead.

The coast to the south of Howick was still unspoilt as far as I could recall. There were no lights to be seen, although of course it would be close to one o'clock now and everyone would be in bed.

As I waded closer to the shore, I could see that I was approaching a creek flowing in a narrow stream of muddy water from a deep cleft in the surrounding hills.

The mud was very soft, and by the time I had walked out of the water I was sinking almost to my knees in the wretched stuff. There was a lot of shell in the mud and I knew from the eeling trips of my childhood that the sharp edges would be cutting my feet to ribbons, softened as they were from hours in the water.

Eventually, the estuary mud flats became harder, allowing me to pick my route more carefully, using what light the moon provided to navigate a course to the dark grass land to my left.

Paralysed with cold, my feet smarting from the cuts and utterly exhausted, I climbed a two foot shelf of clay and lay thankfully on the cold wet grass.

My forged passport and the two thousand dollars in notes were intact in my pocket. I couldn't see if the ink in the passport had withstood the soaking but Bernhardt's Polaroid photograph appeared to be all right. I could still make it to the air terminal if I wanted to.

Conway and Monroe would already be trying to force Karen to tell them where the gold was. I wondered what she would say. The truth was utterly unbelievable and, even if she told them about Bernhardt and his roll of paper, I had doubts that the Americans would listen seriously.

She would be better off if she were to lie, saying I'd hidden it somewhere and that she was ignorant of its whereabouts. If she tried that — and I knew she was smart enough to realise that some such story would at least buy her some time, Conway and Monroe would have to contact me in order to exploit Karen as a hostage.

Meanwhile, the police now knew we'd revisited Marine Parade, unless by some chance the incident hadn't been linked with us. That was very unlikely — they knew all right, and my desperate run for freedom must have confirmed their suspicions that we were responsible for Boyd's murder. It was ironical that the very existence of the two Americans was probably unknown to the police, while Karen and I, who had done nothing, were being hunted down like a couple of criminals.

If the Americans wanted to trade Karen for the gold, we would have to establish contact, which meant one or other of us coming out into the open. They must know there was danger for me from the police, and it was reasonable to suppose they would make an attempt to get in touch by some means or other. I wondered if they would go up north to their cottage.

Of course, it was possible they would be afraid I might spill the beans about David Wendle, and they would know I could also go to the police and accuse them of being responsible for the murder of Boyd Hallett. The whole thing was too complicated, all I could hope was that they wouldn't mistreat Karen in their efforts to obtain information about the dust.

The longer I thought, the less serious Karen's position seemed. Perhaps the Americans would be more reasonable than I first feared. They'd murdered Karen's brother and now her husband — but killing her as well could serve no purpose. That started me wondering why Boyd had been murdered at Waihi and raging uncertainty started to make me feel sick again.

I could think of no solution to my problem. One thing was certain — I couldn't stay here forever letting my mind go round in circles. If the police had any sense at all they'd have their dogs out at daybreak, combing the shore line north and south of Howick hoping to find where I'd landed.

It seemed more sensible to find some way of hiding until, either I hit upon some definite move I could make or the Americans came up with a way of contacting me. How the hell they were going to do it, I didn't know, but what alternative did I have? To make matters worse, if Karen had told them the truth about the gold they would have no further use for her and I would never hear from them. I could imagine what that would mean for Karen.

Tortured with my thoughts, realising the helplessness of my position, I decided that before daylight I was going to steal a boat and take off into the loneliness of the Gulf. An unimaginative and timid plan, but the best I could think of.

15

On the shore, most of the mud flats had been covered by the incoming tide now, making it much easier to distinguish between dry land and silt.

My brief rest had allowed me to establish a few rough details of my plan to steal or borrow a boat. Expensive yachts or launches would have to be avoided. The owners of such craft could be reasonably expected to keep a watchful eye on their investment and understandably create a hue and cry if it disappeared one night.

Identification would be too easy in a large boat as well.

My choice must be the simplest, cheapest and most innocuous hulk I could find — one that was not going to be missed. This of course was assuming I could find any boats at all.

The creek did not appear worth exploring. It might be navigable by shallow draught rowing boats or canoes, but I couldn't imagine anyone keeping one tied up along the banks.

Putting my shoes on, I began paddling my way further south.

A low shelf of clay at the water's edge assisted my progress considerably, allowing me to slither along at what I thought would be about two miles an hour. Using this estimate, I travelled for a little over three miles before encountering another larger estuary, also bounded by extensive areas of shell and mud not yet covered by the tide.

The creek before me appeared to be almost a hundred yards wide, opening gradually at its mouth as it wound its way out to open water. To my right, inland a little way, masts of differing heights clustered together in the dark as if for company.

Where there were yachts, there would be dinghies — or better still, proper rowing boats.

Heartened by my good fortune, and sinking deeper into the mud at each step, I moved slowly along the edge of the small waterway until I drew level with the main body of the crafts.

Mercifully, I was not going to have to swim again. Pulled up untidily onto the shell beach were a number of small boats for me to choose from.

Some were too heavy to drag to the water, others were obviously not seaworthy and some were even chained and padlocked to the neighbouring boundary fence posts. Three were suitable but none had rowlocks or oars.

After wasting a lot of time, I eventually abandoned my search for an elusive pair of oars. Leaving my clothes, which by now were quite dry, in a pile on the beach, I took reluctantly again to the water, swimming the short distance to the nearest yacht. It was a pretty little keeler about twenty-four feet in length but the cockpit was empty and the hatches firmly locked.

Using logic born of long experience, I struck out next for the boat I would have visited last by choice. Needless to say, a pair of oars lay on the bunk nearest the aft hatch — not a good pair — but I didn't need good ones.

With one under each arm I propelled myself awkwardly back to shore where, shivering again, I put my clothes on over my clammy skin.

Two short lengths of rotten cord improvised as rowlocks for my twelve-foot clinker-built craft and I even managed to borrow a small spade anchor attached to about six feet of new polypropylene rope. The rope would have made very reliable rowlocks but I had no means of cutting it.

Once afloat, the tide quickly began to tug me inland and I had to row powerfully to make any headway at all. When I had left the narrow confines of the muddy river, the drag on the hull decreased, allowing me to settle to an easy regular stroke.

Rowing had never been one of my stronger sports, however, it was not long before the shore became indistinct, and I felt as though I was far enough into the Gulf to adopt a complete southerly course to take me further away from Auckland's coastal suburbs.

Periodically, I rested my aching shoulders, wondering if it was the old hurt in my back that was bothering me or a completely new pain. Sitting in the boat on the now slightly choppy sea, I chilled very quickly. A slight breeze was blowing making rowing much easier than it had been previously. Despite this assistance, progress was dreadfully slow and without being able to stop myself, I became overcome with self pity over the loss of the girl I loved so much. Out here in the loneliness of the Gulf, my plight seemed insuperable and Karen gone forever.

It was the first definite rays of the morning sun that made me take a hold of myself.

For some time it had been obvious that the darkness was lifting, the horizon beginning to lighten to my right allowing me a much clearer view of the islands and mainland.

Then, later, with astonishing rapidity, the tip of the huge ball of fire crested one of the dark islands, flooding the Gulf with a wash of brilliant white light. I stopped rowing to watch, aware that I was gaining heart as more and more of the sun climbed out of the horizon.

Soon it was impossible to look any more. My eyes were already drunk and watering from the magnificent spectacle. With renewed vigour I bent my back into the job, watching the swirl of water as each oar pushed against the sparkling morning sea.

With my spirits higher than at any time since leaving Howick the night before, I resolved to row until I was unable to pull another stroke.

My intended destination lay somewhere below Kawakawa Bay, the beach that Karen and I had visited during our daily trips away from the motel at Papakura. The coastal population there has always been very small, being confined to small groups of holiday houses at places that could be easily reached by road.

Perhaps only half way there my soft hands let me down. With my socks padding the grips of the oars, I rowed more slowly now until the freshening wind began to carry me still further into the lower reaches of the Gulf.

Washing the wool fibres from the raw flesh of my hands in salt water was an extremely painful experience and I knew I would be unable to row much further — even if circumstances demanded it.

The day passed by slowly as my craft continued to move under the action of the gentle breeze. I became both hungry and thirsty but concern for Karen occupied my thoughts for most of the day.

The choice between sitting up in the boat and using my body as a sail and lying down where it was warmer was made easy throughout the afternoon, but, with the advent of evening, I stretched out on the boards at the bottom of the hull in order to shelter from the rapidly cooling wind.

My progress towards the Firth of Thames was most satisfactory. I drifted along, watching the sky deepen in colour, then counted the stars one by one as they appeared — abstractedly noting the difference from the night sky of the northern hemisphere.

Doubting my ability to navigate accurately in the dark, and knowing my sense of time would be impaired by my inactivity, at what I judged to be eight o'clock, I began to steer myself shorewards again.

Using one oar as a rudder and waiting to see if the faint coastline drew closer, I strained my eyes towards land.

My crude effort at steering was working, although it was too early to know if I was going to make it without rowing. The tide was helping me too and the wind hadn't become a gale as I had feared it might.

Half an hour later, my ordeal by sea, if you could call it that, ended by running into a line of rocks that jutted from one side of a curved beach. I had been intent on steering for the centre of the pale strip of sand and had quite neglected to watch out for hazards.

No damage had been done though; the collision would have been more serious if I'd been moving fast, but at my gentle rate of drift, the sturdy craft had probably sustained no more than a small dent in her woodwork.

Glad that this time my landfall was on sand as a change from glutinous mud, I was soon dragging the boat up onto the foreshore wondering what daylight would reveal of my surroundings.

I had dozed a bit during the earlier part of the evening whilst laying in the bottom of the boat, but it hadn't helped reduce the fatigue that some hours ago had begun to creep over me.

Rather than using the anchor, I tied the painter to a handy pohutakawa tree and climbed a steep path to a grassy plateau some fifteen feet above sea level.

There was no dew. The wind that had blown me here had kept the long coarse grass quite dry during the early hours of the night.

I spent half an hour making a poor excuse for an open air bed, wrapped myself in a crudely woven mesh of bracken and fell asleep at once.

* * *

The hollow empty feeling about Karen caught up with me within ten or fifteen seconds of waking up. Before that, although the time period was so very brief, the beauty of a New Zealand shore at early morning swamped everything.

A couple of mynah birds were quarrelling in a nearby tree. Perhaps they were arguing about the sudden appearance of the strange thing in the grass. I whistled at them but it made no difference to their squawking.

The wind of the night before had disappeared, leaving the sea almost dead calm. My beach was beautiful, as beautiful as the ones I used to invent when describing New Zealand to my Canadian friends.

Exploring the clearing where I had spent the night soon loosened up my muscles, and the short walk seemed to put most of my worries into perspective too.

A stream trickled out of the cliff close to where I had left the boat. The water looked clean enough and tasted excellent. Later I would follow the little water course inland, just to check that there wasn't a dead sheep decomposing in it somewhere. It is always as well to be sure of such things.

From the promontory of rocks I gathered enough mussels in ten minutes to provide me with an adequate breakfast. I had never eaten them raw before and hoped I wouldn't have to again. Quite obviously cooking alters their flavour completely.

Before establishing a permanent or semi-permanent base I had to determine how exclusive my beach really was — it was important to make sure I was not going to be disturbed.

Using a coarse rectangular search pattern, I explored a region approximately half a mile square without discovering any sign of habitation.

Secondary growth had been cleared on some of the hills further inland and there was a brand new wire fence stretching over a hump between two gulleys. Someone was breaking in the land up there but they weren't going to bother me.

After winding about all over the place, my stream vanished into a tangle of native bush. I abandoned my check after only fifty yards. If I could boil water I would, but if that was impossible I wasn't going to worry very much.

Satisfied that the beach was mine alone, and secure in the knowledge that there was no one to wonder what I was doing there, I began to build a proper camp.

Using the leaves from nikau palms, tree fern branches and flax, I soon constructed an acceptable shelter.

An axe or even a pocket knife would have allowed me to make a more elegant structure but as I had only my own hands, and sore blistered ones at that, I was forced to improvise, using lengths of driftwood for the main frame. I had plans for obtaining some basic necessities later, but right now it was important to have somewhere to sleep in the event of rain.

When the bivouac was finished, I gathered plenty of dry firewood and some kindling which I stacked inside around the thick mattress I had made from fern and bracken.

I remembered a remark I'd made to

Peter Crittall in San Francisco — something about going bush and lying around on beaches this summer. November was a little early for it, but here I was — just as I'd promised. The circumstances were rather different to those I had anticipated.

It was past midday before I was satisfied with my camp — too late to discover the best way to the nearest road. Tomorrow, weather permitting, I would have to find a village store where I could buy a few simple but essential items of equipment. It was also important for me to keep in touch with the outside world if I was going to hear from the Americans.

As usual, my plan was simple. Putting myself in their place, and assuming Karen had been as smart as I prayed she would be, Conway and Monroe had to contact me somehow or other. I would remain hidden at my camp for the bulk of the wait, making periodic trips to the nearest point of civilisation only for supplies and for the purpose of viewing the newspapers each day.

The remainder of the day was spent busily in a variety of ways. I gathered more mussels from the rocks and dug two shoes full of tua tuas from the beach, placing them in a pool just above high water together with some lengths of fresh Neptune's necklace — the only edible seaweed I could remember.

A fragment of beer bottle stubbornly refused to focus the sun's rays onto a pile of dry leaves, meaning I would either have to eat raw shellfish again this evening or go hungry. Previous experience at making fire using friction prevented me from even attempting to try the process on this occasion. Tomorrow I could buy matches and I knew they worked.

Before darkness fell, I collected a number of young coiled tree fern shoots and some puwha, a non-prickly thistle which is a favourite of the Maoris. Both are excellent cooked, but, eaten raw leave an unpleasant taste in the mouth — the fern shoots having a sticky juice and the puwha being extremely bitter.

In my pocket was the two thousand dollars that Bernhardt had given to Karen and me. I would have gladly exchanged it all for a cigarette.

16

I nodded to Tom Bradshaw using what had become my customary method of greeting.

'Gidday Jim,' he said. 'Did you have that bit of rain up in the bush last night?'

With water still dripping onto the floor of his store from my clothes and with my boots caked with mud, I felt disinclined to answer.

'Don't know how you jokers can stick it in weather like this,' he said grinning at my bedraggled appearance.

This was the fourth day I had called at Bradshaw's store. On the first morning I had introduced myself as Jim and had not needed to enlarge on my name since then. My brief explanation that I was 'possum hunting on a block of Government land way out over the back of the hills had been accepted without question, Tom Bradshaw proving most obliging during my routine morning visits to his tiny store.

He produced a large polythene bag. 'Better put your tucker in here for the trip back.'

I said, 'I only want a couple of cans and some bread thanks — beans'll be fine.'

I took the morning paper from the pile on the counter, scanning the headlines while he packed up my small order and changed the ten dollar bill I gave him.

'Are you sure that's all?' he asked. 'You don't need any more gear or anything?'

Three days ago, when I'd first arrived at Orere Point from my camp, I had managed to buy almost everything I'd needed from Mr. Bradshaw's store. My boots, my jacket and my shirt had all come out of the tiny room at the back of the shop, and all at most reasonable prices too. Finding Tom's General Store had been a real piece of good luck.

The village or township of Orere consists of one dairy, one general store and numerous summer cottages, the majority of which are only used at weekends in the hot season. Permanent all year round residents are few, and it was rare for me to encounter anyone else in Orere during my short trips between the edge of the bush and the store.'

I said, 'Maybe I'd better take some more cigarettes — I guess some of my supply might have got wet — the hut's not much good in real heavy rain like last night.'

I turned to the Personal Column of the newspaper. As usual there were only a few inches of entries. But this morning, there it was at last. Just as I'd expected.

'Would Mr. Robert Morgan of St. Heliers Bay telephone Auckland 103-496 where his wife Elizabeth is anxious to hear from him.'

Tom Bradshaw was saying something to me.

'What?' I asked.

'I said how many packets — that's all — don't look so surprised mate.'

'Oh — two will be enough thanks.'

After my days of awful frustration, and those sleepless nights wondering what had happened to Karen, it was wonderful to have my doubts removed by the three lines of newsprint.

She was alive — my decisions had all been right.

I thanked Tom Bradshaw for the groceries, left the store and walked quickly to the phone box just down the street.

The receiver shook slightly in my hand as I asked the operator for the number. Conway answered.

I said, 'This is Robert Morgan speaking — I'm calling in reply to your advertisement in this morning's paper.'

'Ah, Mr. Morgan, we've been waiting for you.'

'Is my wife there?' I asked.

'I am a close friend — able to speak on her behalf.' He sounded smug.

I said, 'Unless I can speak with her first, I'm not prepared to talk to you or anyone else.'

There was a pause and then, 'All right buddy.'

Heart beating I waited. Then Karen's voice sounded breathlessly in my ear. 'Robert, oh Robert darling — you're all right?'

'I'm fine, but what about you?'

'I'm okay too — really I am. I've explained that you can help my friends find some property they've lost, all I know is you left it somewhere near Paeroa — '

I interrupted her. 'And if I take them to it, you won't have to stay with them any longer?'

'Yes, that's right.'

So Karen had fooled them, exactly as I thought she would.

'Let me speak to Conway again — but before I do that, I want to say it's all going to be okay and I love you.'

Conway came back on the line at once.

'Okay Morgan, you understand the deal?'

'Yeah, I understand.'

'Where are you?'

'That's my business.'

'You'll have to meet us if you want your wife back.'

'And you better be more careful on the telephone for all of us.'

He was quiet for a moment after that.

He said, 'Where will you meet us?'

'I want Elizabeth first.' I thought it was worth a try.

'You're not that stupid, Morgan.'

'Then you can't be stupid enough to

expect me to hand over without guarantees can you?'

In fact, in my optimistic moments whilst camping on the beach, I had foreseen this difficulty of transfer. There seemed to be no obvious solution other than one of the parties agreeing to trust the other. I had no intention of trusting the Americans, their record was much too poor to even consider it.

Conway seemed determined to make the deal right away.

He said, 'We'll give you the address here and you can phone Elizabeth when you've handed the stuff over to us.'

I hoped like hell the exchange wasn't listening. The conversation wasn't turning out to be exactly guarded. Any local telephonist would have her headphones burning a hole in her head by now.

I said, 'Not a chance, I don't trust you.'

'Then what the hell do you suggest?'

I said, 'I have a plan which should be agreeable to you.'

'Let's hear it.'

Trying to sound as though I didn't care

whether they liked it or not, I explained the scheme.

I said, 'Tonight, at any time you choose, leave a car for me to use at Orere Point — my wife'll tell you where that is. Park outside Bradshaw's store and leave the key under the carpet on the passenger side at the front. Tomorrow morning I'll meet you at the intersection of a dirt road that goes to a place called Golden Cross and the main Thames-Paeroa highway.'

'What time?' Conway asked.

'I don't know exactly, my watch isn't going — say ten o'clock.'

'What happens when we meet you?'

'I take you to the stuff and we make the exchange.'

Conway laughed shortly. 'You don't mind giving it all away then?'

'I'm sick of it — you're welcome — all I want is Elizabeth back.'

I hoped that sounded convincing over the telephone.

'Are you at this place Orere now?' Conway asked.

'No,' I lied, 'but I can get to it without too much trouble.'

'So if we get you a car you'll meet us tomorrow?'

'Yeah. Can I speak to my wife again?'

'No.'

The phone clicked, ending the conversation abruptly.

I had set the stage, all I had to do now was to act out my part, making sure that I made no mistakes in pulling off a hundred and fifty thousand dollar confidence trick to rescue Karen.

* * *

On the following morning, the walk from my camp to Orere seemed much longer than usual. I had experienced a feeling of regret at leaving my beach which, for the past few days, had been my home. Perhaps Karen and I would return there one day, although I knew that for years to come New Zealand wouldn't be a safe place for us. Anyway, such thoughts were premature. We still had to reach North America and I knew the next few hours might well prove to be the most important in my life.

A pale blue Cortina was parked outside Tom Bradshaw's place. I knew it was mine.

Hoping he wouldn't see me — I was in no mood for early morning pleasantries — I slipped quickly into the driving seat and slid my hand under the rubber mat for the key.

As I drove, my thoughts centred on the few minutes that must pass when the four of us would stand looking at the excavator.

Knowing there was no gold there, Karen would be expecting me to have an ace or two up my sleeve to get us out of the mess. Only I knew there was no gold and no aces either.

I had toyed with the idea of taking the Americans to some other spot, but I didn't know of one that would be convincing, and the quarry seemed to be as good a place as any for a showdown.

At what I estimated was remarkably close to ten o'clock, I rounded the curve in the main highway to see the Chrysler parked across the mouth of the unsealed metal road. The boot lid was badly crumpled.

I parked beside it with all the doors in the Cortina safely locked from the inside.

Karen was sitting in the back seat, smiling at me through the closed window but looking pale and frightened.

Monroe was sitting in the driving seat, his face more ugly than I remembered it.

Winding down my window I said, 'It's not far from here.'

Conway stretched across the car from the passenger seat to talk to me.

He said, 'It's sure nice to see you again Mr. Gallagher — we were afraid the law might have caught up with you a while back.'

I said, 'Why did you kill Boyd Hallett?'

'To find out where the dust was.'

'You don't get information from a dead man.'

'We didn't intend to kill him.'

'Like the accident with David Wendle?'

'Shall we get on and collect the gold Gallagher — then you and Mrs. Hallett can be reunited — you can at least feel free now that Boyd isn't in the way any more.'

Really meaning it, I said, 'You're a bastard.'

'The gold, Gallagher — the gold.'

'How do I know you won't pull a gun on me when we get there and kill both of us when I've shown you where it is?'

'Why should we do that?'

The question was unreasonable. Karen and I were the only two people who knew Conway and Monroe were responsible for the death of two men. It would be convenient to silence us, but I knew that could make things more difficult for the Americans. Not only would our deaths be unexplained should our bodies be found, but it would automatically remove suspicion from us for Boyd's murder. Anyway, I had no choice but to hope for the best and keep on my toes.

I said, 'Drive up here a mile and a half then turn left down a track all overgrown with gorse. You can't miss it — there aren't any others. Two hundred yards down, there's an old quarry with a rusty digger sitting in the middle of it. The gold's in four bags under the belly.'

Monroe spoke for the first time. 'Aren't you coming with us?'

'Right behind you.'

'Why not in front?'

'Because I'm nervous.'

That seemed to go down okay.

Monroe started the car, turning the front wheels harshly on the loose gravel before accelerating up the road in a cloud of fine yellow dust.

I followed, wondering if the hole in the ground left by Bernhardt and myself where we'd taken out the bags, had subsided with the recent rain.

Now I was beginning to tense up badly. The moment of truth was not far away. Until I knew what the Americans wanted to do, I couldn't formulate any plan of action. Once we had got out of our cars at the quarry, there would be only minutes for me to decide what to do.

Reversing the Cortina into the quarry would have been a better idea, but for the fact that I thought it would raise unnecessary suspicion.

They were waiting for me.

I got out and leant against the car.

I said, 'I want Karen out too.'

'When we've got the gold.'

'I've told you where it is.'

'Show us.'

I pointed to the excavator. 'Over there.'

From where we stood the shallow depression in the clay appeared quite obvious to me, but I didn't think the Americans had seen it yet.

Conway said, 'Don't be childish — you come with us.'

'Not unless you let her out of the car.'

I could see he was becoming impatient.

He said to Monroe, 'Get the girl out and stay here with her — I'll go with Gallagher.'

That didn't help me at all. If both of them had walked to the excavator with me, perhaps there would have been a remote chance for Karen to have got away, leaving me to handle the Americans. Now, because of my stupid insistence about her being allowed out of the Chrysler, Monroe was going to stay here.

My mouth was dry with fear and my legs were unwilling to move forward.

I said, 'Go on then, let her out and I'll take you down.'

Monroe opened the car door, pulling

Karen out by her wrist.

I snarled at him, 'Go easy — she's a woman.'

Karen's eyes were wide as I walked past her to join Conway already on his way to the excavator.

When I caught up with him I said, 'I hope you go to hell with the gold round your neck.'

He ignored the remark, continuing his brisk walk to the rear of the old digger. The hole in the clay stood out like a sore thumb.

Turning round to face me he said, 'You're sure it's here?'

'There's the hole,' I said, nodding at the ground in front of him.'

He was looking suspicious now.

'Yeah — a hole not a bump.'

'Try it,' I said, moving slightly forward.

As Conway started to kneel down to begin his digging, I hurled myself at his back, forcing his body violently forward onto the rusty steel.

With a tremendous blow, his forehead hit the flat plates on the left-hand track of the excavator. Simultaneously my fist exploded into the side of his face.

I had tried to kill him but hadn't managed it by a long way.

He was on his knees moaning, his right ear split wide open from the blow from my fist. But he certainly wasn't dead.

With a hundred yards between me and Monroe there wasn't time to finish the job.

Spinning round, I sprinted towards the man and woman by the car. Monroe was already moving.

Before I'd covered a quarter of the distance he had raced round to the boot of the Chrysler to reappear with a rifle in his hands — my Marlin.

I saw him pump the lever and raise the weapon, just before I started my first weave to the left.

The crack of the shot exploded into the confines of the quarry, but there was no fiery bite of a high velocity shell tearing its way into my soft body. I was sure he wouldn't try to kill me. With me dead their chances of recovering the gold would be gone for good. If he was only trying to frighten me he was succeeding only too well.

Turning back to the right, knowing the closer I got the easier it would be for him, I saw that Karen had the barrel in both hands, with her small body curved over the rifle. Monroe was hitting her on the back and trying to wrench the weapon from her grasp.

She was on her knees by the time I cleared the ledge onto the track in one giant leap.

I met Monroe with six inches of steel sheath knife in my hand — one of my purchases from Bradshaw's store.

He saw it in time, side-stepping neatly, leaving Karen and the rifle in a crumpled heap on the ground.

Bouncing off the Chrysler, I turned to face the big American.

He had his jacket wrapped round his left forearm as a guard and crouched ready for me.

In the distance, Conway was staggering towards us.

Feinting with the knife didn't fool Monroe. He still waited.

Thrusting forwards with the short knife I nearly overbalanced as he leapt back.

On two feet, his recovery was quicker than mine and in an instant a massive hand clamped round my wrist and began to twist. His strength was enormous.

Like a nightmare, the pointed tip of the blade slowly followed a curved path backwards towards my own stomach.

I tried to drop the knife but couldn't.

In one last desperate heave, I attempted to twist my body clear. Simultaneously Karen swung the rifle inexpertly by the stock, sinking the blued steel barrel into the American's thick neck like a piece of cheese wire.

The grip on my wrist relaxed at once as Monroe fell to the ground gasping, his eyes glazed with the sudden pain.

I grabbed Karen, pulling her roughly towards the Cortina.

She climbed in, still dizzy from the beating as I slammed my door shut and started the engine.

Both Americans were on their feet, moving towards their own car and watching me begin to reverse down the track, trying desperately not to get wedged into the high clay bank.

Even before we'd cleared the worst of the gorse I heard the roar of the exhaust as the Chrysler engine started.

Knowing I should have kicked Conway's head solidly into the steel tracks and left my knife in Monroe's guts, I turned the car onto the gravel road and pushed the pedal hard onto the floor boards.

17

With her head on my lap, Karen was sobbing, 'Oh God, oh God — take me away, Russ,' as I slid the car straight out into the main road hoping fervently that there was nothing coming.

Letting the engine howl until the valves bounced, with all my weight, I slammed the lousy column shift into each gear as quickly as the lever would move.

Using the whole width of the road where I miscalculated our speed, in a series of shrieking power drifts and largely uncontrolled slides, we screamed between the rock walls of the gorge, sweeping over narrow bridges and accelerating to maximum speed before braking violently for the next sickening group of bends.

How Karen stood it as a passenger I could not imagine. After a while she recovered sufficiently to sit up.

She said shakily, 'I seem to remember us doing something like this once before.'

Through clenched teeth I said, 'I wish we had the Zephyr this time.'

We were through the gorge now, and under normal circumstances the road would have been regarded as much better, the twists and turns giving way to gentler curves with short straight sections in between.

The Cortina would just about stagger up to eighty miles an hour on the speedometer, but the acceleration after slowing for a corner would be no match for the big Australian engine in the car behind.

'Go to a farmhouse, Russ — people will help us.'

'Not if Conway and Monroe tell them we're wanted for murder they won't.'

'But we can't just keep on driving — anyway look at the gas.'

Despairingly I saw the gauge reading only quarter full. Not that it would make much difference, I couldn't hope to outrun the Americans. There was a chance I could keep them behind us by blocking the road for a while, but in the end either they'd get by or I'd lose the

Cortina completely and we'd end up in a twisted heap of bloody metal.

I said, 'They think if they lose us this time, they'll have lost their chance of ever getting hold of the gold.'

Suddenly the Chrysler appeared in my mirror — just for a moment before the curve of the road hid it from view again.

Karen shouted at me over the engine's roar soon afterwards.

'Can you see them yet?'

'Yes I can.'

Setting her features she said, 'If you brake as hard as you dare round the next corner and leave the car across the road there'd be enough time for us to get out wouldn't there?'

'Just about, I suppose' — I wasn't keen on the idea.

'Well?'

'If we get out and they manage to miss the Cortina they'll have us cold — I don't feel like fighting the pair of them again.'

Karen shook her head. 'We could block the whole road.'

'Not in a hell of a hurry we couldn't — it's a pretty wide road and after the sort of stop we'd need to make I couldn't guarantee to end up sideways in the right place. There wouldn't be time to mess about either — we'd have to be out the instant the car stopped — even then we mightn't make it.'

I had to speak in single sentences, pausing in order to concentrate on my driving.

It was obvious that we couldn't continue like this for much longer. Miraculously I had been on the right side of the road when passing the only two approaching cars that had been encountered so far — the third might be the last one we'd ever see.

Postponing the inevitable seemed stupid. I slowed to a safer speed, waiting for the Chrysler to roll round the last bend behind us.

Monroe was driving again. I saw his surprise when the gap between us narrowed at an alarming rate — he even had to brake slightly.

For the next minute or so he kept the car close behind us, not attempting to pass. Karen refused to look over her shoulder.

At the beginning of the next straight Monroe tried to get by. The manoeuvrability of the larger car was no match for the Cortina. A flick of my steering wheel was all that was needed to block his lane. No matter how quickly he swerved, it was simple to place my car in the way in an almost leisurely fashion — Monroe had no hope and he knew it.

Suddenly there was movement in the front seat of the Chrysler. 'Get on the floor!' I yelled at Karen wrenching the steering wheel violently to one side.

Conway had the Marlin in his hands.

I didn't think he'd try and shoot us — he'd never get the information he wanted that way, but it would be simple enough to hole our gas tank or put a bullet in one of our rear tyres.

I had to spend nearly all my time looking in the mirror watching Conway's progress with the rifle. He was leaning out the window now. When he steadied the weapon I yanked on the wheel again. Just in time.

The bang was louder than I'd anticipated but he must have missed by several feet.

Karen reappeared from the floor. She said, 'I'm not staying there — I feel sick as well as scared — did he miss?'

'By a mile, but he'll try again.'

But our luck changed. The friendly shape of a milk tanker appeared ahead.

'Now what?' Karen asked. 'What in God's name can we do now?'

'Stop in Paeroa in the busiest place I can find — there's nothing they can do there without causing all sorts of trouble.'

'But they can still say we're wanted by the police.'

'Don't forget there's plenty of police there — if Conway and Monroe try and get us arrested properly, they won't get any information out of us. They can't pull any rough stuff either.'

We were up close behind the tanker now. I intended to stay there, hoping another vehicle might catch up with our convoy. All I had to do was to keep the Americans behind us until we reached Paeroa.

In fact, Paeroa was but a mile further on. Safely sandwiched between the tanker and the Chrysler which was soon followed by a light pick-up which joined the queue just before entering the township, we drove at twenty miles an hour into Paeroa's main street.

Choosing an obviously busy side road, I turned left, leaving the tanker to lumber on its way. Monroe must have been watching closely — the Chrysler followed as though it was on rails.

Half-way along the block I had to take avoiding action to miss a battered old Vauxhall which shot out of an alley between two shops. The large Maori driving the rusty car was as startled as I was. Unknowingly, he gave us our first real chance by conveniently stalling square in front of the Americans.

I accelerated, turned right along a narrower street and turned right again. And then suddenly there was the answer.

The alley from which the Vauxhall had appeared earlier was a through route from the street we were on now. I could see a one way sign ahead, and beside it our means of escape.

Lifting the wheels on the Cortina, I lurched violently into the protection of the little alley, braking to a halt as soon as I could. At the same time I was yelling to Karen.

'Get out — come on — come on.'

I pulled her to the green taxi, opened the rear door and tumbled in on top of her to the astonishment of the sleepy driver. Galvanised into action by our obvious haste, he had the engine started and the car moving in no time.

'Where to?' he asked over his shoulder.

'Just keep going out of town towards Thames,' I said, holding Karen down on the back seat where I had pushed her.

'Stay there for a bit,' I whispered.

Leaning forward to speak to the driver with a handful of dollar bills, I glanced into his driving mirror but could see no sign of the Chrysler.

I said, 'For money — how far can you take us?'

He offered me a cigarette, squinting sideways and noting my beard, the result of several days ineffective shaving at the beach using my knife.

I must have passed the inspection — or maybe it was the dollars.

'For money,' he said, 'as far as you like.'

'Then I should like you to take us nice and gently to a place called Orere Point.'

'It'll cost you my return trip too.'

'I know that — I know it'll be expensive.'

He passed me the cigarette lighter from the dashboard.

He smiled — 'Be glad to take you mister — tell your girl friend she can get up — there ain't nobody behind us.'

Karen was flushed — it was nice to see some colour in her face after the frightened pale countenance that had persisted since the episode at the quarry.

She slid across the seat, put her arms round my neck and kissed me hard on the mouth.

For several miles, the driver carefully avoided looking in his mirror, leaving us to make up, at least in part, for a lot of lost time over the past few days.

When we came up for air, he turned to nod at Karen.

He said, 'When I get a job like this, it's hard not to ask for the story.'

'For another cigarette, our story is

yours.' I'd left mine in the abandoned Cortina.

I said, 'Would you believe we're eloping?'

'Whatever you say.' He passed me the packet.

'It's like this — '

Improvising, with Karen filling in with some very imaginative detail, I spun a yarn about shotgun wielding brothers who couldn't understand that sisters well over twenty-five knew who they wanted to sleep with. We made it spicy enough to keep him full of interest for over half the trip.

When we had finished recounting our tale, he remained quiet — thinking no doubt that we were heading for trouble in a big way. I thought it might have been more amusing to have told him the truth just to see if he believed it.

It was late afternoon when he dropped us at Orere. I thanked him very much, giving him a ten dollar tip for his trouble. He shook his head slightly — as if in amazement — when he said good-bye and wished us luck.

'This is where you've been staying?' Karen queried.

'Not exactly — but near here. You and I are going to spend a few days at my camp whilst we organise new airline tickets.'

A terrible thought seized me.

'Have you still got your new passport?' I asked her anxiously.

She waved her handbag at me. 'In here.'

'Didn't the Americans want to know where it came from?'

'Of course they did. I told them you arranged it all — they think you're pretty smart.'

As we still had our passports, and I still had plenty of cash, there appeared to be no reason why we shouldn't carry on with our original plan. In the morning, I would ask if Tom Bradshaw could arrange to pick up a couple of reservations for us when he went into town next.

'This way,' I said to Karen, pulling her across the small side street leading to the trail to my private beach.

I had to help her in places, the ground still being slippery from the rain where it was unprotected by the stands of huge fern which lined each side of the crude track to the coast.

When we reached the top of the rise, I pointed downwards to the distant yellow strip of sand.

'That's it,' I said.

The feeling of security began to return as soon as we descended to the sea.

My shelter made Karen giggle.

'What's so funny?' I asked her.

'I feel rather like a city girl who's married an out-back farmer and is viewing the homestead for the first time.'

'Do you feel newly married?'

'Yes I do rather.'

'I thought you might have got over it at St. Heliers.'

'Don't you want to make love to me here?'

I didn't answer that in words.

* * *

Afterwards we lay in the long grass of the plateau overlooking the beach, exchanging information about our experiences over the past few days.

Conway and Monroe had taken Karen directly to the beach house at Whangaruru North where I'd been chained up as a prisoner. There, and on the drive north, they had questioned her about the gold. Although very frightened, she had lied well, convincing them that they would have to get hold of me in order to discover where I had hidden it.

The first night they were there, Monroe had threatened to rape her if she didn't tell him the truth, but, by sticking to her story and pretending to be utterly terrified, which wasn't difficult, she had managed to persuade him to leave her alone. To reinforce her position, she had suggested that I might not be as willing as they supposed to exchange the gold for my girl friend.

Conway seemed to think I was something of a hard character, and was reluctant to try anything too serious on Karen in case I got mad and decided to keep the gold after all.

Apparently, the only suspicious moment

occurred when I had agreed on the telephone to give them all of the dust in exchange for Karen. Both men had expected to have to bargain for part of it, not believing I would consider relinquishing the whole three hundred pounds.

It had been Karen who had suggested returning to Auckland and placing the advertisement in the paper for me, telling the Americans that I would recognise the name Elizabeth Morgan because of the passports I had obtained for us.

I told Karen of my escape from Marine Parade in Howick, realising as I spoke that the police would have had an impossible job trying to find me once I'd swum out to sea.

When it was dark, I lit a small fire on the beach inside a circle of large stones, over which we cooked an evening meal using cans of food taken from my supply.

The fight at the quarry seemed much longer ago than this morning as we sat together on the rocks, watching the flickering flames of the fire. I felt more alive and happy than I had done for many a long and anxious day.

For a time we said nothing, listening to the gentle lap of the waves whilst I held Karen in my arms, stroking her long hair and breathing the fragrance of her and of the cool night air, realising there was nothing else I would ever need now.

Later, absorbed with each other, we climbed the path to the clearing where we squeezed side by side into my tiny bush shelter. There, with our bodies pressed together, we drifted into a sleep of contentment, each of us caught by the spell of the other and each of us with our emotions swamped by our new found happiness.

18

The two mynah birds that had been arguing on my first morning at the beach had arrived again to inspect the new resident.

I went to see if the fire could be revived. The night had been dry and the rocks surrounding the black embers were still warm, but there was no sign of any smoke.

Nevertheless, the empty bean tin full of clear water from the stream was soon surrounded by the glow from burning pohutakawa twigs and coffee was only minutes away.

Karen ran down the path towards me, her hair flying loose behind her in the sunlight and the glow of a fresh morning on her cheeks.

'What's for breakfast?' she asked brightly.

'There's canned fruit, canned fruit juice, canned meat and fresh coffee.'

'No canned cereal and milk or canned bacon and eggs?'

'Only canned milk — I forgot to mention it.'

She skipped on to the sea, laughing as a wave caught her by surprise and splashed the front of her skirt.

I watched her, wondering that her presence could make me feel so different inside.

When we had eaten our rather strange meal, sharing my knife as the only utensil we had between us, Karen went to bury the empty cans leaving me to prepare for my trip to the store at Orere village. She had wanted to accompany me, but I had thought it would be more sensible and safer for her to stay at the camp. Tom Bradshaw would be expecting me and I wouldn't be away very long.

She said she would improve the shelter and make it fit to live in, joking about my low standard of housekeeping.

Walking through native New Zealand bush is a pleasant experience — even if the going is hard. There is a quietness and a friendly solitude that is not apparent from the outside. This morning, I enjoyed my trip more than any other walk that I could ever remember.

I had convinced myself that we would be able to fly to America in a matter of days now. The hue and cry for Russ Gallagher and Mrs. Karen Hallett might still be on — even intensified after my brief appearance at Howick — but with Bernhardt's passports and the other slight changes we could still make to our features, I didn't anticipate any problem.

Tom Bradshaw was standing in his doorway.

'How are you there Jim?' he said.

'Good thanks — all the better for the sunshine too.'

His attitude was different somehow. I sensed an unusual wariness.

His next remark shook me to the very core.

'Is your second name Morgan then?' he asked pointedly.

'Why?' I said wildly. 'For God's sake why do you ask me that?'

'Couple of jokers here first thing when I opened up — said they was looking for

Robert Morgan.'

'But you know my name's Jim.'

'They described you pretty well mate — said they wanted to talk to you.'

'How did they know I was here?'

'How would I know — Jim or Bob or whatever your name is — they said something about a taxi driver in Paeroa.'

I cursed my own stupidity — why the hell hadn't I realised that the persistence and intelligence of the Americans would have made it an easy matter for them to put two and two together and come up with a taxi.

Trying to keep calm I asked, 'Tom, where are they — the two men — where did they go?'

'I told them you'd be up in the bush over that way somewhere. Are they really mates — you look a bit more than worried?'

'How long ago — I mean when did they leave here?'

'Oh — about an hour — maybe less.'

I turned and began running, a desperate alarm ringing in my head.

For too long I had been dogged by

these men — this time I was going to finish things for good. Part of my building anger was the result of the incredible way in which they had relentlessly pursued Karen in order to use her as a bargaining device. Wherever I went, whatever I did, they turned up to chase those four bags of yellow dust. Their indiscriminate murders for the relatively small sum of money involved branded them as criminally ruthless and brutal animals. They were killers for money and vicious uncompromising bastards. If they had touched Karen this time, they were dead men.

I knew it wouldn't be difficult for them to find my trail — especially on the wet ground. Karen's footprints would be there too. The only trick was finding the beginning. It was even possible that they could have waited for me to appear and then trace our camp back from there. If they'd done that they had something like a quarter of an hour headstart. I had to get back to the beach — back to Karen.

Wondering if they would spring me somewhere along the trail didn't slow me down. I was quite certain they were after

Karen again and probably believed the gold was hidden at my camp.

I reached the rise very quickly, sparing a few seconds to glance down at the distant beach before starting to run and slide down the incline to sea level. There was no sign of anyone on the section of the shore that I could see from the hill.

By the time the ground flattened out, my breath was hot and dry in my throat from the exertion. Now, only a few hundred yards from the camp, I slowed down in order to reduce the noise of my passage through the brittle stands of young trees. I needed surprise on my side for I had little enough advantage as it was.

Emerging cautiously from the bush to the edge of the clearing, I scanned the entire area but still there was no one to be seen. Karen must be down on the beach. I prayed she would be there alone.

Feeling calmer now, I walked past the bush shelter to the edge of the cliff, reaching the sandy beginning of the steep path to the shore just as I heard the first choking cry.

Two more steps were enough for me to see the drama spread out on the sand below me.

Conway was launching my rowing boat through the miniature surf whilst Monroe was trying to drag Karen from the rocky edge of the beach. Her dress was torn and she was struggling helplessly against the strength of the big man.

At the top of my voice I yelled, 'Monroe.'

He looked up briefly.

Karen shouted, 'Russ,' and began trying to free herself with greater effort.

Pent-up fury flowed to my head in one long searing wave of hatred. It was the scene at the quarry again but intensified.

In a few huge bounds, using the heels of my boots to carve their own landing steps in the path, I reached the beach in a flurry of sand and soil.

Using every ounce of the power in my legs, pushing my feet against the loose sand and with pure hate urging me on, I ran for Monroe.

I think that this time he knew I was going to try to kill him.

From the corner of my eye I saw Conway leave the boat and start running, carrying one of the long oars with him.

When I was twenty yards from Monroe, he pushed Karen roughly away and bent to pick up my Marlin rifle from the rocks beside him. He was frightened this time — I could see it in his eyes as he levelled the weapon at my legs and pulled the trigger.

As he had at the quarry the day before — he missed — the bullet landing somewhere in the sand between my feet. The expression on Monroe's face grew more frightened as the distance between us narrowed.

Frantically he moved the lever on the Marlin, knowing there would be no time for another shot before I reached him. This time he didn't aim at my legs.

A fraction of a second before he fired, almost at point blank range, Karen pushed herself suddenly away from the rocks and launched her body at the American.

I caught her in my arms at the instant the rifle went off, the blast throwing her backwards towards me.

Below her breast, an insidious dark stain spread at an alarming rate over the tattered material of her dress.

Monroe still held the rifle, his hand in the action of levering another cartridge into the breech.

Letting Karen slide to the ground from my arms, I stepped over her form and grasped the Marlin with both hands — one around the barrel, and the other just in front of the trigger guard.

In a matter of seconds Conway would arrive. There was no time left.

Using strength born of animal hatred for a deadly opponent, I brought my knee up violently between Monroe's legs, watching his face contort with the terrible pain. His grip on the rifle relaxed at once.

I turned swiftly to meet Conway. There was just time.

I shot him twice. Once through the stomach and once through the heart.

Clutching his groin with both hands, Monroe was writhing on the ground screaming when the echoes of my shots stopped bouncing off the hills.

Trembling, my legs weak, but still holding the rifle, I knelt in the sand beside Karen. Her breathing was very laboured and her eyes were closed.

Gently I touched her face with my hand.

'Russ,' she whispered without opening her eyes, 'Is that you?'

'You're going to be all right,' I said with my face close to hers. 'Everything's going to be fine.'

Her lips moved again. 'Russ — he would have killed you.'

'I know that — you saved my life.'

The blood was all over her dress now, the redness just beginning to stain the sand on which she lay. Surprisingly the wound did not appear large, although I was going to have to stop the bleeding and get her to hospital at once.

Karen opened her eyes.

She said, 'Russ darling — kiss me.'

I bent nearer but her head lolled sideways before I touched her lips.

'Karen,' I said wildly. 'Karen.'

She was dead.

I stood up. From the hip, at a range of

eight feet, I emptied the rifle into Monroe, riddling his jerking body with bloody holes.

Then with all my remaining strength, I hurled the Marlin into the sea, lay down with my head on Karen's warm body and cried for the life of the girl who had meant more than life itself to me.

Around me, tiny waves turned red as they ran back frothing towards the sea.

I didn't want to wake up, but the hostess was insistent.

She said, 'I'm sorry sir, but we'll be landing shortly and you must fasten your seat belt now.'

Mechanically I did what I was told, my mind refusing to accept the facts of what had happened.

Over and over again I had mentally re-enacted the scene at the beach — my beach — the most beautiful beach in the Gulf. It was better to be asleep with my nightmares.

I don't know how long I lay on the wet sand there, letting the tide come in to wash the blood away.

When I at last picked up Karen, the

bodies of the men I had shot had been taken by the tide and the beach was quiet.

That afternoon, and all that night, I cradled the body of the dead girl in my arms, knowing that the promise of life which was to have been ours was no more and that it was my own greed that had wrecked the future forever.

The next morning I left the camp, stumbling somehow to a road where I was picked up, exhausted and still wet, by a passing motorist who delivered me to Auckland without asking questions.

There I pulled myself temporarily together, bought a single ticket to Montreal and flew out of Mangere Air Terminal many hours ago. I experienced no trouble of any kind in leaving the country.

In Los Angeles I had phoned Bernhardt who had driven out to see me immediately. Over a cup of coffee I told him of the dreadful ending to the story and refused to accept the cheque and tape recording he had brought with him. I think he understood.

Before he left we had shaken hands like

two close friends. Only he would ever know the awful truth about the tragic and brief return to my homeland.

Later, I had considered calling in to see Bev and Peter, but couldn't bring myself to impose my misery on them again. No one could help me this time.

★   ★   ★

From my seat in the 707, the lights on the ground could be seen through the window now. In a few minutes I would be back in Canada.

I gathered my travel documents together, wondering if the police would meet me at the exit of the terminal.

Then, with the other passengers, I filed out of the plane, ready to walk across the flight apron to the building.

Gallagher, Brackenridge, Morgan — who I was didn't matter now. Nothing would ever matter again.

Outside it was snowing hard. The temperature was a bitter two degrees below zero and it was autumn.

We do hope that you have enjoyed reading this large print book.

Did you know that all of our titles are available for purchase?

We publish a wide range of high quality large print books including:
Romances, Mysteries, Classics
General Fiction
Non Fiction and Westerns

Special interest titles available in large print are:
The Little Oxford Dictionary
Music Book, Song Book
Hymn Book, Service Book

Also available from us courtesy of Oxford University Press:
Young Readers' Dictionary
(large print edition)
Young Readers' Thesaurus
(large print edition)

For further information or a free brochure, please contact us at:
Ulverscroft Large Print Books Ltd.,
The Green, Bradgate Road, Anstey,
Leicester, LE7 7FU, England.
Tel: (00 44) **0116 236 4325**
Fax: (00 44) **0116 234 0205**

Other titles in the
Linford Mystery Library:

DEATH CALLED AT NIGHT

R. A. Bennett

Jimmy Ellis believes his parents have died in a car crash when as a young boy he is taken to live with relatives in Australia. The years pass happily, then the nightmare comes. Terrifying images flit through his mind in the dark — all through the eyes of a child, a witness to grisly events seventeen years before. He begins to delve into the past, and soon he finds himself on the trail of a double murderer — a murderer who is prepared to kill again.

THREE DAYS TO LIVE

Robert Charles

Mike Harrigan was scar-faced, a drifter, and something of a woman-hater. With his partner Dan Barton he searched the upper reaches of the Rio Negro in the treacherous rain forests of Brazil, lured by a fortune in uncut emeralds. Behind them rode three killers who believed that they had already found the precious stones. And then fate handed Harrigan not emeralds, but the lives of women, three of them nuns, and trapped them all in a vast series of underground caverns.

DEATH IN RETREAT

George Douglas

On a day of retreat for clergy at Overdale House, a resident guest, Martin Pender, is foully murdered. The primary task of the Regional Homicide Squad is to track down the bogus parson who joined the retreat. Subsequent events show that serious political motives lie behind the killing, but the basic lead to it all is missing. Then, three young tearaways corner the killer in the woods, and a chess problem, set out on a board, yields vital evidence.

THE DEAD DON'T SCREAM

Leonard Gribble

Why had a woman screamed in Knightsbridge? Anthony Slade, the Yard's popular Commander of X2, sets out to investigate. Furthering the same end is Ken Surridge, a PR executive from a Northern consortium. Like Slade, Surridge wants to know why financier Shadwell Staines was shot and why a very scared girl appeared wearing a woollen housecoat. Before any facts can be discovered the girl takes off and Surridge gives chase, with Slade hot on his heels . . .

SEA VENGEANCE

Robert Charles

Chief Officer John Steele was disillusioned with his ship; the *Shantung* was the slowest old tramp on the China Seas, and her Captain was another fading relic. The *Shantung* sailed from Saigon, the port of war-torn Vietnam, and was promptly hijacked by the Viet Cong. John Steele, helped by the lovely but unpredictable Evelyn Ryan, gave them a much tougher fight than they had expected, but it was Captain Butcher who exacted a final, terrible vengeance.

HIRE ME A HEARSE

Piers Marlowe

Whenever Wilma Haven decided to be wayward, she insisted that she was seen to be wayward. So perhaps she was merely being consistent when she hired a hearse before committing suicide, then proceeded to take her time over the act in a very public place. However, Wilma died not from her own act, but by the murderous intent of an unsuspected killer, and Superintendent Frank Drury of Scotland Yard becomes embroiled in his most challenging case ever.